## "Why did you agree to this meeting?" he asked, his skepticism searing.

"Because I have another proposition."

"Uh-huh. Let's hear it," he said. Taking the bait. *Finally.*

"I will lease you the land you require for your resort."

"A lease is no good to..."

"For one hundred years with all requisite permissions to develop it that you may require, as long as you stick to Androvia's strict rules on sustainability," she countered before he could sidetrack her again. "But on one condition."

His frown leveled off. "Go on."

She took a steadying breath, let it out slowly, and—feeling oddly exhilarated—forced herself to let go of twenty-two years of caution and control, so she could finally take charge of her own, and her country's, destiny.

"You agree to marry me, Mr. Lord."

## By Royal Arrangement

*Two royal households...both alike in infamy!*

The Queen of Androvia must find a husband...or submit to a dynastic marriage to the playboy prince next door!

Innocent Isabelle is certain there couldn't be a more scandalous match for her than Prince Rene. So, when she meets American billionaire Travis Lord, she has an outrageous proposition for him. She'll let him build his exclusive Androvian resort—if he'll marry her! Then she gets a taste of her new husband's total disregard for protocol...and the scorching chemistry between them. Has she leaped from the frying pan and into the fire?

Find out in
*Queen's Winter Wedding Charade*
Available now!

Notorious royal Rene from the neighboring principality once shared a secret night of passion with Androvian lady-in-waiting Mel, but there's been an icy rift between them ever since. Now a New Year's Eve Ball results in a shocking twist of events: Rene and Mel have disappeared...together!

Read all about it in Rene and Mel's story, coming soon!

# QUEEN'S WINTER WEDDING CHARADE

## HEIDI RICE

**Harlequin**

## PRESENTS

**Harlequin®**
**PRESENTS™**

Recycling programs
for this product may
not exist in your area.

ISBN-13: 978-1-335-93941-8

Queen's Winter Wedding Charade

Copyright © 2024 by Heidi Rice

For questions and comments about the quality of this book, please contact us at CustomerService@Harlequin.com.

TM and ® are trademarks of Harlequin Enterprises ULC.

 Harlequin Enterprises ULC
22 Adelaide St. West, 41st Floor
Toronto, Ontario M5H 4E3, Canada
www.Harlequin.com

**Printed in Lithuania**

MIX
Paper | Supporting
responsible forestry
FSC® C021394

*USA TODAY* bestselling author **Heidi Rice** lives in London, England. She is married with two teenage sons—which gives her rather too much of an insight into the male psyche—and also works as a film journalist. She adores her job, which involves getting swept up in a world of high emotions; sensual excitement; funny, feisty women; sexy, tortured men; and glamorous locations where laundry doesn't exist. Once she turns off her computer, she often does chores—usually involving laundry!

## Books by Heidi Rice

### Harlequin Presents

*Revealing Her Best Kept Secret*
*Stolen for His Desert Throne*
*Redeemed by My Forbidden Housekeeper*
*Hidden Heir with His Housekeeper*
*Revenge in Paradise*

### Billion-Dollar Christmas Confessions

*Unwrapping His New York Innocent*

### Hot Winter Escapes

*Undoing His Innocent Enemy*

### Billion-Dollar Bet

*After-Party Consequences*

Visit the Author Profile page
at Harlequin.com for more titles.

To my sister-in-law Isabel, whose wonderful hospitality I enjoyed while writing this book and who is a queen in her own right. xx

# CHAPTER ONE

'HER ROYAL MAJESTY, Queen Isabelle of Androvia is ready to see you now, Mr Lord.'

Travis Lord turned from the spectacular view of spruce and pine forests and virgin snow through the mullioned window, to find an old guy in fancy velvet knickerbockers and enough braid to sink a gunship standing behind him.

*About damn time.*

'Cool,' he said, hiding his mounting irritation behind a relaxed smile, because he guessed it *was* cool, in a weird way.

When was the last time a guy from a trailer park in Snowton Colorado got an audience with a queen? Even if he did have more money now than the oldest of Alpine monarchies.

'Let's go,' he murmured.

The guy bowed then directed him out of the antechamber he'd been waiting in for a solid twenty minutes and into a large salon, which, according to Travis's research, was just one of the White Palace's ten staterooms.

Luckily Travis had spent his whole life not being impressed by unearned wealth—and the sort of people his mom had once cooked and cleaned for—so he managed to contain his awe. But it was more of an effort than usual.

Because the collection of antique furnishings, the vintage oil paintings adorning every wall, and the fanciful gold-plated plasterwork—not to mention the even more stunning view of the Alpine gorge the palace perched on the edge of through six enormous floor-to-ceiling stained-glass windows—made one hell of a statement. In fact, the impressive décor looked like something out of a Disney princess's palace. Probably because this bastion of old-world elegance—a six-hundred-room, three-centuries-old ice-cream castle, which towered over Androvia's pristine slopes—was the real-world equivalent.

After walking the length of the gleaming parquet flooring, the courtier led Travis up a wide marble staircase. 'You have been briefed on the etiquette when greeting Her Majesty, sir?' the man asked as they stopped in front of a carved mahogany door.

'Sure,' Travis replied, humouring the guy.

No way was he executing the bow he'd been advised to do—he was an American, and his ancestors had fought a war so they didn't have to bow to anyone—but he wasn't about to get booted out before he'd met the woman he'd flown eight thousand miles to see.

He wanted to buy a piece of her kingdom for Lord Culture's first European resort and from their research Queen Isabelle might be in the mood to make a deal. She had wealth, and lots of it, but it was all tied up in historic properties like this one, fancy bits of jewellery and the other antique collectables that came with a legacy dating back to the sixteenth century—all of which cost a fortune to maintain and operate. What she didn't have was disposable income. Plus, his intel suggested she was also having a spat with her Ruling Council over the future of the monarchy itself.

They wanted her to 'merge' with the heir to a neighbouring kingdom—one of those Eurotrash princes who played hard and didn't seem to work at all—while she was holding out. Travis Lord could take the pressure off by bringing jobs and investment to her country.

This was a business proposition between equals—so no bowing was required. But he kept that to himself as the courtier nodded, then tapped on the ornate door. A muffled voice told them to come in.

Travis stepped into a large library, which smelled of old paper and lemon polish, the walls covered in bookcases, with an antique desk at the far end.

The young woman sitting behind it, her blonde hair pinned up in a ruthless updo, was a surprise—especially when she stood and walked towards him. Instead of velvet and ermine and the crown he had been expecting, she wore a tailored pantsuit which was probably supposed to look businesslike but hugged her figure as she moved. She was also tiny. Or he guessed the word was petite. She barely reached his collarbone. She looked a lot taller in her press pictures. Her heart-shaped face, wide, slightly sloping green eyes and porcelain skin also made her look younger than her twenty-two years. Her make-up was subdued, conservative even, but instead of making her appear regal and reserved it made her seem oddly innocent—like a teenager who wasn't yet ready to advertise her charms, instead of a woman in her early twenties, who had to be well aware of the effect she had on men. His gaze tracked to her mouth—the pale pink lip gloss couldn't disguise how lush her lips were… A bolt of lust shot straight into his groin. And he tensed.

*What the hell?*

'Your Majesty, Mr Lord to see you as requested,' the

courtier—who Travis had forgotten was there—announced while executing another deep bow.

'Mr Lord, we meet at last,' the Queen said in perfectly accented English, her voice a soft purr of privilege and purpose.

She didn't offer him her hand in greeting.

Travis yanked himself out of the fugue state he had lapsed into unintentionally, and managed to stop fixating on her lips long enough to figure out she was probably waiting for him to bow, too.

*Yeah, not gonna happen.*

The courtier cleared his throat, obviously thinking Travis had been struck dumb by his first encounter with royalty—which, annoyingly, wasn't far from the truth.

Travis ignored the prompt. 'Your Majesty, you're a hard woman to get an audience with,' he said, then offered her his hand. 'But it's good to meet you at last.'

The courtier gasped. Travis ignored the guy some more.

The Queen glanced at his open palm. If she was surprised, or even annoyed, by his refusal to follow protocol though, she managed to contain it and hesitated for less than a second before accepting the handshake.

Her palm was cool, and her fingers long and elegant, but her small hand disappeared in his much bigger one. Her tiny jolt of surprise, the little frisson of electricity, echoed in his groin.

Was he getting turned on? Weird, but kind of intriguing, too.

He released her hand, but then caught a lungful of her scent—and wondered how something so subtle could be so intoxicating.

The courtier had stiffened up like a poker, his outrage at the break in protocol emanating off him like a force field.

The Queen sent the guy a polite smile and he melted like a snowman on a Florida beach. 'Arne, could you leave us now?' she said. 'And tell Mel we'll be ready for the tea tray in twenty minutes,' she added.

She turned to Travis, the polite smile becoming politely inquisitive. 'Unless of course you would prefer coffee, being an American?'

'Coffee works,' he said, trying not to get dazzled by the smile—which managed to brighten her whole face despite her reserve.

'We can dispense with the titles now,' she said, as soon as the courtier had disappeared. 'I'm afraid Arne worked for my father and he's a terrible stickler when it comes to protocol.'

Travis nodded, relieved. Being unexpectedly turned on by this woman was one thing, having to treat her with fake deference was another. Maybe she didn't consider him to be an equal, but she was well bred enough not to show it—which was good, because he didn't really give a damn what she thought of him. He'd never let anyone's opinion of him—high or low—stop him getting what he wanted.

She directed him to a leather armchair in front of her desk. 'Please take a seat, Mr Lord, we have a lot to discuss.'

He detected the tight tone and noticed the polite smile had left the room with Arne the Stickler. *Interesting.*

He took the seat she suggested and watched her walk back around her desk and sit down. Her movements weren't quite as fluid as they had been when she'd walked towards him, nor as precise. Seemed Her Majesty was a little tense. *More interesting.*

'So, I take it you know why I wanted this meeting?' he said, deciding to cut to the chase.

Fast and direct was how he rolled. It was the way he'd ridden a snowboard to a gold medal in the world championships as a teenager and made his first billion while creating his own brand sportswear in his twenties. He'd also told his negotiators to give the Queen's advisors a heads up while they'd been angling for this meeting. As interesting as it had been meeting the woman in the flesh—and getting a glimpse of how European royalty lived—he hadn't come here to sightsee. Or genuflect.

She gave a stiff nod. 'You wish to acquire a three-thousand-acre portion of Androvia's White Ridge to build a ski resort. Land which has belonged to the royal household for ten generations and has remained untouched.'

'That's about the size of it, yeah.' He leant forward, surprised she was being equally direct, but also impressed by the shrewd intelligence in her gaze. He hadn't expected her to be a pushover, but he also hadn't expected her to handle the negotiations herself. *Even more interesting.*

'Although it's going to be primarily a snowboarding resort—not a ski venue,' he said. 'And while we want to develop the land, it's the untouched quality of the wilderness which makes it attractive to us. Lord Culture is all about exclusive bespoke resorts which blend with the natural environment. Any construction we do will be ecologically sustainable and supremely sensitive. The idea is to enhance the White Ridge, not destroy it. We give our clients unique wilderness experiences. Our two resorts in the States are award-winning and speak for themselves.' He took a breath, then went in for the kill, because straight talking was one of his superpowers. 'Plus, we both know you're between a rock and a hard place at the moment, Your Majesty,' he added, enjoying the way she stiffened even more.

'How so?' she asked, the prim tone not matched by the flash of fire in her eyes. So, the Queen had a temper, good to know.

'A deal of this size with Lord Culture will bring thousands of much-needed jobs to your subjects and substantial investment in your infrastructure and will also give you, personally, increased financial clout. Enough so you won't have to contemplate hooking up with the playboy prince next door if you don't want to.'

Isabelle jolted with shock at the audacious—and far too personal—observation.

She'd met Americans before, she knew they didn't tend to stand on ceremony, but she'd never met anyone as forthright as Travis Lord.

She'd thought she'd been prepared for this meeting. She'd done her research after all, as what she had to suggest to this man had to be managed *very* carefully.

But the minute the former snowboarding champion and billionaire entrepreneur had strolled into her study, she had begun to wonder if she had bitten off a lot more than she would ever be able to chew. For starters, Travis Lord was enormous. Lean and muscular—as befitted a man who had once reached the pinnacle of a dangerous and demanding sport—but also incredibly tall. He had to be at least six four when she was only five three in bare feet. And while she'd known he wasn't a small man, and had worn her highest heels to compensate, even so, he made her feel exceptionally short.

The feel of his callused palm, closing over hers—the

scrape of roughened skin, the warm dry flesh—had been supremely disconcerting too. Even that brief contact had made sensation sprint around her entire body. And that was before she had factored in the question of why exactly she had given in to the impulse to shake his hand in the first place. The whole concept was completely alien. But when he'd offered his palm, something untoward had come over her and she'd had the unprecedented desire to take up the dare. Because that was exactly what she had seen in his eyes—the warm hazel flaring with provocation, challenging her to allow him to demolish centuries of protocol less than a minute after meeting her.

She'd also been prepared for his striking appearance. She'd seen the many photos of him over the years. First as a teenager, taking every title and breaking numerous records with a reckless natural talent that had dared fate at every turn, until he'd fallen to earth in a brutal accident that had almost cost him his life at the age of only nineteen. But he had risen from the ashes of his athletic career in his twenties, modelling his own skiwear, which had become North America's most sought-after brand within a decade.

Now he was in his early thirties, his looks had matured from the sun-kissed athletic beauty of his youth to a supremely masculine handsomeness. His features, once so finely drawn, were now weathered by a scar on his cheek and another that slashed across one brow, not to mention the break on the bridge of his nose. His dark wavy hair was glossy but needed a trim, being long enough to curl against the collar of his shirt. And while the designer suit he wore was perfectly tailored to all those muscles—the man obviously kept in shape even if he was no longer a professional sportsman—the expensive fabric still only barely contained his rugged physique.

What she hadn't expected though were for his looks to have such a profound effect on her. She'd met good-looking men before, but she'd never had the urge to stare at one… Or, indeed, allow him to shake her hand.

And then there was his scent, which she had got far too intimate an acquaintance with as he had loomed over her. Not expensive cologne, but clean cedar soap underlaid with something musky and even more compelling.

She had been taught from a young age to keep a ruthless leash on all her emotions, and never to let her reactions show. But something had overwhelmed those years of training from the moment he had walked into the library.

As she stared back at him now, trying to compose herself after his shockingly inappropriate comment, she realised the brilliant scheme she had come up with late at night, over many months, after stressing about the prospect of having to consider marriage to Rene Gaultiere, the neighbouring Prince of Saltzaland, might not be so brilliant after all.

She'd assumed she would be able to make this man an offer he couldn't refuse and then control the outcome. She wasn't anywhere near as confident about the second part of that equation now. But as his audacious comment echoed into silence and his dark eyes narrowed, the masculine challenge—and dominance—in his gaze reawakened the strange compulsion which had prompted that ill-advised handshake.

Struggling to channel it rather than succumb to it this time, she delivered the line she had been rehearsing for weeks. 'That being the case, I have a counter offer.'

He didn't look surprised, but then she hadn't really expected him to, as she had already gathered he was even better at controlling his reactions than she was. Either that or he'd had all semblance of sensitivity ironed out of him long ago. A distinct possibility, given his difficult upbringing—as the child of a single mother who had cleaned lodges in an expensive ski resort in Colorado while living miles away in a trailer park. She'd found no reference to his father in the press clippings.

'You haven't heard what I'm willing to offer you for the land yet,' he said, not taking the bait. *Yet.*

'I cannot sell you the land, Mr Lord,' she said. On that much she had to be clear. No Androlov had ever sold off any of the kingdom, it was the royal family's heritage and, as the last of her line, she did not intend to be the first to break that tradition. It was why she was being forced to think outside the box—*way* outside the box.

'Then why did you agree to this meeting?' he said, his scepticism searing.

'Because I have another proposition.'

'Uh-huh. Let's hear it,' he said. Taking the bait. *Finally.*

'I will lease you the land you require for your resort.'

'A lease is no good to—'

'For one hundred years with all requisite permissions to develop it which you may require, as long as you stick to Androvia's strict rules on sustainability,' she countered before he could sidetrack her again. 'But on one condition.'

His frown levelled off. 'Go on.'

She took a steadying breath, let it out slowly, and—feeling oddly exhilarated—forced herself to let go of twenty-two years of caution and control, so she could finally take charge of her own—and her country's—destiny.

'You agree to marry me, Mr Lord.'

# CHAPTER TWO

'I BEG YOUR PARDON, ma'am?' Travis growled, finally managing to contain his astonishment—and the uncomfortable jolt of lust—long enough to form a coherent sentence.

Had the Queen of Androvia just proposed to him? Because that was what it had sounded like. But maybe the twelve-hour flight here from Colorado was messing with his hearing—he sure as heck hoped so.

'You are absolutely correct to suggest Androvia needs investment, Mr Lord,' the Queen replied in a calm, measured voice, as if they were still discussing a land deal, and not something totally nuts. 'And my people desperately need the employment opportunities a resort such as yours would offer. But the only way to allow a construction of this nature on the White Ridge is for you to marry me because the ridge, like all Androvia's royal real estate, is held in a trust, which stipulates any development can only be authorised by a man of royal birth, in other words a king, or by a queen if she is married.'

*Not hallucinating, then. Damn.*

'I am assuming, of course, you have no royal heritage of your own,' she added, her tone clipped and condescending.

'Funnily enough, no,' he said, his own tone caustic.

He wasn't ashamed of his heritage, or rather the lack of

it. His old man had been a rich guy, but he'd been married to someone else when Travis's mom had fallen for the bastard as a teenager and then fallen pregnant. But so what? Travis had never wanted the guy's wealth, or his acknowledgement. He hadn't needed it. Because he'd done just fine on his own.

The Queen didn't seem aware she had insulted him though—because her expression barely changed as she started to outline her nutty scheme.

'Then marriage to me is the only way you would be allowed to build on the land. Or I would be allowed to let you,' she said, still in that matter-of-fact tone. But then he noticed her gaze wasn't meeting his and her posture had stiffened.

Maybe the controlled indifference was a bluff? Why that gave him a rush he had no idea, but he'd take it, if it meant he could regain the upper hand.

'Hold on,' he said. 'Who the hell has the power to stop you doing what you want if you're the Queen?' he asked, because he was beginning to smell a rat. 'Androvia is similar to a constitutional principality, like Monaco, right? You're the head of state and the Ruling Council run the government, but you still own all the land.'

She would have to be desperate to offer a nobody like him marriage—and that was before they considered the fact he was a stranger, unlike the prince next door.

'I see you've done your homework,' she said, clearly surprised he'd bothered. He bristled, but he let it go. He was used to people underestimating him. And it usually worked in his favour.

'In answer to your question, as I am the monarch I am the beneficial owner of the land, but I cannot break this trust, as it was set up by my father, to protect me, when I was still a child,' she said.

His frown deepened. How the heck did stopping her from having authority over her own financial affairs just because she wasn't a guy, or married to one, protect her, exactly?

'I believe my father felt an alliance between myself and Prince Rene would be good for both our kingdoms and he wished to facilitate that. But I'm sure if he had lived long enough to know me as an adult, he would have realised I am capable of making intelligent decisions about the land on my own.'

Despite the telling lack of emotion in her voice as she spoke, something flashed in her gaze, when it met his then flicked away again. He wasn't sure what that something was—disappointment maybe, confusion perhaps, even unresolved grief.

The pulse of sympathy pushed against his chest. Hadn't both her folks died in a helicopter crash when she was still just a kid?

But the something was gone again so fast, his sympathy evaporated.

Whatever issues she had with her old man's refusal to trust her just because she was a girl weren't his business. Being orphaned as a kid was tough, but he'd lost his mom too when he was still a teenager, and he'd survived. And prospered. Plus, it wasn't as if Queen Isabelle had ever wanted for anything. If you were going to get orphaned, better to have it happen in the lap of luxury.

'Okay, so you can't control your own land without getting married,' he said, determined to establish the facts here. 'But if you need a husband so bad, why not just hook up with the guy he wanted you to marry…then lease the land to me?'

While the playboy prince sounded like a loser, she had to at least know the guy.

'Because the Prince and myself are not compatible in any way,' she said swiftly, her gaze direct now and impenetrable, but the colour on her cheeks blossomed.

'And you think *we* are?' he countered, ruthlessly controlling another inconvenient shot of lust.

Seriously? She might be beautiful and one hell of a challenge to a guy like him, which was weirdly hot, and, sure, the White Ridge had been his first choice by quite a wide margin to locate Lord Culture's first European resort… But marriage was way too drastic a solution to close this deal.

Maybe European royalty didn't have an issue with using sex to sweeten business deals but he sure as heck did.

Marriage had never been part of his game plan. He enjoyed good hard sweaty sex, and lots of it, when the chemistry and the timing were right. And companionship, up to a point, as long as it didn't get in the way of his work commitments. But he had never believed in hitching your future to someone else's star—thanks to all the losers he'd watched his mom hook up with over the years, starting with the bastard who had got her pregnant at seventeen then hightailed it back to his wife…

But even if Travis *had* been the marrying kind and hadn't been deeply cynical about any relationship that required more than supplying his dates with an orgasm—or two—her proposal would still be nuts, because they'd only just met. Literally.

'Our compatibility is completely immaterial,' the Queen replied tightly, throwing him even more. How exactly was a marriage between them supposed to fly when they knew not one thing about each other?

'Uh-huh,' he said. Was she really going to make him state the obvious?

Seemed she was when she only stared back at him, clearly waiting for him to make the next move.

He took his time, checking her out—man to woman. Her eyes narrowed, and her chin lifted, her expression one of pride and no small amount of indignation. He smiled at her reaction, appreciating the way her full breasts pressed against the tailored blouse she wore as her breathing accelerated.

*Tough luck, Belle baby, you started this.*

He refused to relinquish eye contact, rewarded when the blush spread up her neck. He relaxed back into his seat, starting to enjoy himself—the shift in power from her back to him almost palpable.

Yeah, Her Majesty might be an accomplished diplomat, and stateswoman, used to getting her own way despite her current fix. But he'd hazard a guess she was a lot less used to propositioning guys, especially guys like him, who weren't at her beck and call.

'It may be immaterial to you,' he said, eventually. 'But it isn't to me.'

Her blush intensified. Yup, this was definitely her first rodeo, marriage-proposals-to-American-roughnecks-wise.

She opened her mouth to reply, but he beat her to it.

'Correct me if I'm wrong, but you've just asked me to hook up with you on a permanent basis. Which makes our compatibility important. Because no way am I gonna agree to marry someone before I know if we're good in bed. And so far, all we've done is share a handshake.'

\* \* \*

Isabelle sucked in a breath. So shocked by the forward comment, she was momentarily speechless.

She had never, in her entire life, been spoken to so disrespectfully. She forced herself to school her features and breathed through the forceful reaction. She must not respond to Travis Lord's attempts to provoke her. Although maintaining her usual composure was not helped by the hot blush currently incinerating her face. Or the rush of blood making the indignation sink into her abdomen—and throb, disconcertingly.

She contemplated her response—and tried to find a positive in the most excruciating conversation she had ever had with a man. Or anyone for that matter.

After several pregnant seconds, she finally managed to control her outrage while attempting to view his candour with as little emotion as possible. Perhaps, his directness was…well, refreshing. At least it meant she could speak plainly, too.

While the man clearly had no respect whatsoever for her position, could she find a way to make that work in her favour? After all, what she had asked of him was the opposite of conventional… Harder to put a positive spin on, though, was the hot brick that seemed to have got wedged between her thighs when he had studied her as if he couldn't see her position, her title, her legacy, all he could see was her. Which was not good. Because the only way to make this proposal work was for her to remain calm and dispassionate with him at all times.

She cleared her throat. 'I think you misunderstand me, Mr Lord. I'm not suggesting a marriage in which…' She paused, aware her blush was probably radioactive by now. 'In which conjugal rights are involved.'

*'Conjugal?'* He spat out the word on an astonished breath. But then his dark brows launched up his forehead, and he laughed. The deep, husky sound made the throbbing worse, even though his amusement was clearly aimed *at* her. 'Are you for real?'

'Of course,' she said, and he laughed again.

What exactly was so funny?

'Is a marriage without conjugal rights not the correct term for a marriage without intimacy involved?' she pointed out. Then realised she'd made another error when he chuckled again—the amusement in his dark eyes turning the hazel to a rich chocolate… Annoyingly.

'Yeah, sure, maybe back in the eighteenth century,' he said, still amusing himself at her expense.

Before she could point out how rude he was being—because, *really*?—he carried on talking. 'So let me get this straight, you want me to marry you, but you don't want me to sleep with you?'

She dismissed the strange pang in her belly—which made no sense whatsoever, because it almost felt like disappointment. 'Of course not, we have only just met.'

And she had never had sex with anyone. She cut off the errant thought before she could give him any inkling of that inconvenient truth.

Her sexual history was hardly relevant. And something about the way he sat in the leather armchair—unfazed by the direction of the conversation, one ankle hooked over his opposing knee as if he were the master of all he surveyed, the smile on his face both knowing and relaxed and far too confident—made her suspect letting him know she was a virgin would only make him more arrogant, and give him more power, when he already had enough. It was more than clear that Mr Lord had a *lot* of experience in the bedroom— something he seemed to be not so subtly advertising to her, quite deliberately—making her sure she was at enough of a tactical disadvantage in this negotiation already.

Unfortunately, it was also a message her body was getting loud and clear—hence the insistent throbbing.

He released his ankle, to lean forward. 'You want to marry me...' he said. 'But you don't want to enjoy it? How is that gonna work...for either one of us?'

She frowned. Was he being deliberately obtuse, or was he just trying to antagonise her? Maybe it was a bit of both. Either way, she tried not to rise to the bait, or get derailed by the over-confident smile and the mocking twinkle.

Maybe this idea had been doomed from the start. She certainly hadn't factored in the extent of Travis Lord's insouciance, his irreverence, his arrogance, his strange sense of humour or his industrial-strength disregard for the strictures by which she had lived her entire life... His very masculine Americanness, basically. But she had become desperate to find a solution to her situation—when it had become apparent that to get her country the development and investment it so desperately needed—i.e. to drag it into the twenty-first century—she would have to either marry Rene or find someone else.

And as far as she was concerned, Travis Lord—for all his faults—was still the better option.

Yes, he was an unknown quantity, but Rene—and a marriage with him—certainly was not. It would be a disaster—Rene was, and had always been, a man much more interested in the reckless pursuit of debauchery than the needs of his kingdom and his monarchy. Plus, Rene would *insist* on a sexual relationship. And expect a real marriage if they were to wed. For the simple reason that, as the last of his line too, he required an heir. And providing one, given his many sexual conquests, seemed to be the only thing he had any aptitude for.

She shuddered at the thought. One day, she would need to think about the continuation of her line, too. But not for a while. And when she did, she intended to take the necessary time to find a suitable match—a man she could admire, who would respect her and her duty. Perhaps she could even find love, the way her parents had once loved each other, but it would not be a dealbreaker. Because her duty to her throne, and her subjects, would always be her paramount concern. So, finding a man she could enjoy a settled, productive life with, who could share the burden of responsibility with her, rule by her side, enrich her kingdom with his wisdom, and be a good father to guide their children to maturity, was a distant goal at this point.

Obviously neither Travis Lord nor Rene Gaultiere would ever be that man. But all she required at present was a husband, in name only, to help her secure her country's future, while also honouring the conditions of her father's will.

'It's fairly simple, really,' she said, determined to take his question at face value and ignore his attitude problem.

'Enlighten me,' he said.

She took another deep breath. Then proceeded to do just that. 'I need a husband to be able to lease you the land. I do not wish to marry Rene, which was my father's preferred choice when he set up the trust. But he did not stipulate who my husband had to be…' *Thank goodness.* 'Or that it was necessary he be of royal blood.'

He was still listening, and he hadn't interrupted. Hope sparked. Maybe this didn't have to be complicated after all. A simple transaction that would give them both what they wanted.

'I can marry anyone. The man does not need to be a prince. Nor does it even need to be a real marriage. But I think, in view of the fact the Ruling Council are likely to be surprised by you as my choice...' because the traditionalists on the council had already dropped enough hints that they considered Rene to be the best option '...it would make sense for us to pretend this *is* a real marriage.' She was starting to babble, but she couldn't seem to stop herself, his silence somehow triggering the nerves that had once made her talk too much as a child on those rare occasions when she'd had her parents' full attention. 'Which would mean us pretending to be in love. For appearances' sake... But given that you are such a successful businessman and you would be bringing a large portion of the infrastructure investment we all want for Androvia with this project, I'm sure the council will come around quickly.'

He nodded. 'I get it. So, you think we can fool the council guys that we're madly in love, while not touching each other?'

She blinked, taken aback by another direct question and the rueful amusement still sparkling in his eyes. Why was he so hung up on the sex bit? When she'd already explained it wasn't relevant?

She forced herself to take a breath, and control her irritation... And her dismay. And give him a straight answer... After all, it was utterly impossible to tell what the man was thinking, so it was probably best not to overthink his question.

'Displays of affection would be necessary in public, to sell the relationship as real. Obviously,' she said, laying her cards on the table—while trying not to imagine those firm lips on hers. 'But it's generally not expected, in royal circles, for a couple to be too...' Her face heated again. *Wonderful!* 'Too demonstrative. So, it really won't be necessary for us to do anything too overt in public. And obviously in private, we would do nothing at all.'

He nodded, slowly. But then his gaze narrowed.

'How long would this marriage have to last?'

The hope blossomed under her breastbone. This could work. He was considering it. The relief alongside that strange surge of sensation was almost palpable.

'I think a year would suffice. After which we could get a divorce. We would of course agree to the terms of the separation in a legally binding confidential contract to protect both our interests before we marry. I believe Americans refer to it as a prenup.' She'd already hired a respected divorce attorney in the US who had agreed to do all the necessary paperwork in absolute secrecy. Because Lord hadn't said anything, though, Isabelle's nerves demanded she fill the silence.

'Fortunately, there is also no stipulation in the conditions of the trust that the marriage needs to last. Just that it needs to be in place for me to make commercial decisions about the land. And a year would give me sufficient time to develop and sign off on a number of other projects, as well as the lease agreement for your resort.'

Her heart thudded heavily in her chest, the sadness—that her father had been robbed of the chance to know her as an adult—springing from nowhere as she conjured up the precious image of his face. He had been so handsome and strong whenever Isabelle had been called into his and her mother's presence as a little girl. She had idolised both her parents, always mindful that their time together was precious, their duties all-consuming. She would never blame him for putting conditions on her accession, which had become increasingly onerous in recent years. She knew he had had her best interests at heart. But she also refused to feel guilty about finding a way around them that would allow her to do her best for Androvia—without having to marry Rene.

'Okay,' Lord said, the amusement in his eyes turning to approval—and making the jolt of adrenaline worse. Which was preposterous. She did not require this man's approval, simply his co-operation. 'That's super sneaky, but I like it,' he said. 'Your old man sounds like a sexist jerk, so it makes sense to game the guy...'

*What?*

Isabelle bit her tongue to prevent her horrified reaction to his thoughtless accusation from slipping out of her mouth.

Travis Lord did not know the first thing about her relationship with her parents, nor did he need to.

'I'm not gaming him,' she said, as calmly as she could. 'I'm simply finding an effective way to fulfil the trust's conditions.'

'Like I said, sneaky.'

She huffed out a breath. And drew it back in sharply.

*Do not let him provoke you, Issy.*

'You're pretty smart, aren't you, Belle?'

*Belle?* She startled at the nickname. And the strange warmth at the thought of anyone using such familiarity. She steeled herself against reacting, though. Even if it was becoming a titanic effort.

'Yes, I am,' she concurred, pointedly, to make it clear his opinions did not interest her in the slightest. Although, to be fair, it occurred to her he looked intrigued now, and impressed, rather than amused, so perhaps that was a good thing.

'So, what do you say, Mr Lord? You pose as my loving husband for a single year, and I will lease you the land on the White Ridge at a very reasonable price, so you can build your resort?'

He leaned back in the chair, crossed his ankle back over his knee, which made the fabric of his trousers tighten across his thigh muscles in disconcerting ways. His searing gaze roamed over her again, making awareness prickle across her skin.

And the throbbing got worse.

She crossed her own legs and tried to squeeze the distracting sensation into submission.

'It's an intriguing offer,' he said at last. 'And I've got to admit, a tempting one. But the answer's no.'

'I beg your pardon?' she said, sure she could not have heard him correctly.

'The answer's no, Your Majesty,' he said, with a finality that shocked her more, and a mock deference that had the spark of temper igniting.

'But… *Why?* This is the only way to give us both what we want,' she demanded, hating the hitch in her voice.

If he refused, she would surely be forced to seriously consider proposing to Rene? Not only did she shudder at the humiliating thought of having to go to him, cap in hand, and beg him to marry her. After she had already turned him down once. But she knew he would absolutely insist on a real marriage. And would probably make her jump through several hoops beforehand, just to pay her back for her previous rejection.

Travis Lord was her only hope of avoiding that humiliation. Because she simply did not know any other eligible men whom she could bribe into a marriage in name only.

'I want the land on the White Ridge, sure,' Lord said with maddening insouciance as her frantic thoughts began to spiral into the abyss. 'But I don't want it *that* much.'

'Would a marriage to me really be so onerous?' she asked, then winced at the note of desperation. She must not let him see how much she wanted this to work, or she suspected he would take advantage and become even more arrogant… And contrary.

'Yeah. Because I'm guessing you'd want me to live here, with you, for the duration of our fake marriage.'

The tension—and panic—in her gut eased.

Perhaps this was a problem with a practical solution, not an outright rejection. A solution she was more than willing to negotiate.

'I'm afraid you would have to reside in the White Palace for the majority of the year, yes,' she said, because that much was non-negotiable. Not only did she need to sell this marriage to the Ruling Council, she wanted to sell it to her subjects too, so they would get behind the construction of the new resort—and the other changes she hoped to bring to the country's infrastructure to help drive economic growth. 'But you would be able to keep up your business commitments. I would endeavour to keep your official engagements to a minimum. And I could certainly make your commitment to me personally worth your while.'

'How?' he asked, bluntly.

So, he wanted to play hardball. She could handle that.

'We could discuss the terms of the lease—negotiate a very favourable rate for your business,' she said, a backup position she'd planned for. The truth was, she'd be happy to lease the land for a lot less than it was worth, if she had to. The investment in the country's infrastructure and the chance to circumvent the trust that had hamstrung her monarchy for so long would be worth it. The preliminary plans his company had already submitted included a heliport and an upgrade to the country's aging rail system as well as over a thousand skilled jobs during the construction alone. But she wasn't about to let him know that yet.

Then he derailed her, again.

'I'm not talking about the money. Or the land.'

'You're… You're not?' she asked, hopelessly confused.

'You really don't see the massive problem here?' he countered. But it sounded like a rhetorical question, which only confused her more.

'No, I do not.' She stared, waiting for him to elaborate, knowing she had exposed herself enough—and also suspecting if she started talking again, her nerves might not allow her to stop.

'If I'm going to live here, for an entire year,' he drawled, as if he were talking to someone who was not all that bright, 'as your loved-up husband, I'm guessing I won't be able to date anyone else, because that isn't gonna sell the "we're madly in love" vibe if the media find out.'

The skin on her cheeks burned, the wildfire spreading across her collarbone, as what he was implying finally dawned on her.

'Being celibate for a year is a problem for you?' she murmured.

'Hell, yeah, isn't it for you?' he shot back.

The blush intensified as she tried to cover her dismay—and the now insistent throbbing at her core.

'Well, obviously, it's not ideal,' she managed, attempting to sound as if she knew what she was talking about, when sexual frustration had never, *ever* been an issue for her. 'But I'm sure I could make the sacrifice worth your while…'

'Oh, yeah? How?' he demanded, the heated purpose in his gaze suddenly making her palms start to sweat. And the throbbing in her core become turbo-charged.

*We could dump the no-sex rule.*

She swallowed down the utterly inappropriate thought that popped into her head—and made her sex clench and release.

What was happening to her? She did not wish to be in an intimate relationship with any man, *yet*. And certainly not with a man like Travis Lord, *ever*. He was far too arrogant and overpowering… Plus, the American billionaire might as well have had 'sex god' tattooed on his forehead, while she was a complete novice. He would almost certainly laugh at her inexperience and could use it against her—when he got bored with her, which of course he would.

She was a queen, not a courtesan. And while she needed this marriage, she had no intention of risking emotional intimacy with any man—least of all a man like him who had already proved to be wholly unpredictable and not any-where near as easily controlled as she had hoped. So, she blurted out the only thing she could think of to keep the negotiation on track.

'What if I offered to lease Lord Culture the land you want on the White Ridge for a single dollar?'

# CHAPTER THREE

TRAVIS STARED AT the woman in front of him, struggling to contain his surprise, and that vague feeling of insult that he remembered from when he was a kid—and he'd had to help out his mom on her jobs, while the rich kids they were cleaning up after looked at him like dirt. This wasn't personal, that much was obvious, so why the hell was he insulted she'd rather sell a tract of her precious kingdom to him for a dollar than consider sharing a bed with him? It wasn't as if he had been suggesting they hook up. But her desperation to get this deal, without going there, still got his goat. And he wasn't even sure why.

The truth was, he'd decided as soon as she'd made the offer not to accept it. Sure, he was intrigued and kind of flattered—at first—that she would ask him. But at the same time, he wasn't about to relocate his whole operation, and sign some secret agreement, or pretend to love someone he didn't know just for a piece of land. He had his pride and, now he was a billionaire, he could afford to keep it.

The White Ridge might be perfect for what he wanted, but it felt as if he would be selling his integrity—along with his time—and, while he'd always been ruthless, even he had balked at the thought of posing as a loving husband when he was about as far from ever being that as it was possible to get. Hell, how would he even pull off the charade she was suggesting, given he wasn't a professional actor? But weirdly, as he had glimpsed emotions that she had been trying to hide flit across her face—shock, confusion, panic—pretending that he wanted her, a lot, hadn't seemed like such a stretch. Because the truth was, for reasons he could not begin to figure out, the whole 'ice princess' act she had going on was a challenge that he found surprisingly hot.

Maybe that explained why he was so mad right now. When he shouldn't be…

'A dollar?' he said. 'Are you serious?'

He'd already decided not to go for this deal… But now he was forced to reconsider. Because more than anything else, he had always been a shrewd businessman. His business had saved him after the accident, when he'd had to give up the sport he loved, and eventually become his life's work. And while he had resigned himself to start scoping out the other places his team had shortlisted before they'd settled on this one, there was nowhere better for the resort than the White Ridge. He had been ready to offer her up to a half a billion dollars for the land. His turnover was enough at the moment he could afford to pay top dollar, but it would still have been a risk—because Lord Culture's brand wasn't yet established in Europe. Getting the land for nothing would take that risk away. And give him the opportunity to invest even more in the construction. And the marketing.

In fact, while he hated to admit it, marrying the Queen would be a huge PR boost, not just for the resort itself, but also for him personally. It would give him class, and an exclusivity he would never have been able to achieve on his own, not just in the States, but globally. And the kind of organic, viral, wall-to-wall publicity that couldn't be bought. It annoyed him he needed to care about that stuff, because he'd never aspired to be anyone other than who he was… But from a business standpoint, he'd be dumb to ignore the opportunity to turn Lord Culture into something more than just the fastest-growing winter sports brand in the market. This deal could send his business over the top. Give him global reach. And seal his legacy for a generation. And for that, he had to consider his integrity—and his hurt feelings—an acceptable price to pay.

'Yes,' she said, staunchly. 'One dollar.'

He stood up. To hell with it, he'd be nuts not to take a deal like this, no matter the pitfalls. And when it came to business he always went with his gut. And his gut was screaming at him right now to take the deal. 'Okay.'

She blinked, several times, her cheeks reddening again. His heart rate sped up. And the heat in his groin pulsed, hard.

'Really?' she asked, momentarily nonplussed. 'You'll agree to the marriage?'

For some reason, he found himself smiling. When he'd walked in here, he'd got the definite impression this was a woman who was well versed in ruthlessly controlling her emotions, and her reactions. That he unsettled her, and seemed to have knocked her off kilter, felt like an important win.

If they were going to spend the next year bonded at the hip, he was going to need something to entertain him—and pushing her boundaries seemed like a great place to start. Especially if he wasn't going to be having any sex—the one recreational activity he really enjoyed, other than boarding.

'Yeah. Have your attorney send the paperwork direct to my EA, Claire Ainsley. She'll handle everything from my end.'

'Excellent.' Her breath gushed out as she came around her desk. Her face brightened, and her expression became unguarded for the first time.

The heat surged.

*Great*, he was going to have to get a handle on that reaction if he was going to deal with her for a whole year. But even as the thought occurred to him, he couldn't resist the urge to poke at her composure again.

'I guess we'll have to figure out a dating itinerary for the next couple weeks. So we can be seen getting up close and personal before you tell everyone how you've fallen madly in love with me.'

'Oh, yes, of course, absolutely,' she said, even though he suspected she hadn't considered doing any such thing— which only made the urge to push more irresistible.

He lifted his hand and traced his thumb down the side of her face. Her brows rose and he felt her vicious jolt of reaction. But she didn't pull away.

His grin widened. 'Perhaps we should practise before I go,' he teased, unable to resist.

'I beg your pardon, Mr Lord.'

'Call me Travis, Belle,' he said, using the nickname he knew had horrified her earlier. He'd used it then to unsettle her deliberately. It had a similar effect now.

'Belle is not my name. It's Isabelle, or Issy,' she whispered. 'That's what my mother called me.' Sadness shadowed her eyes before she could mask it.

'I prefer Belle. It's better if my pet name for you is unique.' He brushed his thumb across her lips. Her eyes widened, and he had the weirdest suspicion she'd never been touched by a man before... But then he got a clue.

She was just skittish with him because she didn't know him.

This situation was super screwed up, whatever way you looked at it, but the sooner she got used to his touch, the better.

'Okay, if you insist,' she said, the intelligence in her eyes dispelling the shock. 'And what should my pet name for you be?' she challenged. 'Trav, maybe. Or Vis?'

He chuckled. Was she making a joke? Because as outlandish as it seemed, it was also kind of cute.

'They used to call me Killer on the slopes,' he said, trailing his thumb down the elegant line of her neck and pressing the pad against the rampant pulse in her collarbone. Still she didn't draw away.

'Killer doesn't seem very romantic,' she managed, although her breathing had become ragged. Her throat contracted as she swallowed, the heat rising like a wall. Tall and infallible.

He was playing with fire. He'd agreed to no sex. But hey, they had to be convincing for this to work, and anyway, when had he ever been the type of guy who denied himself something he wanted...? And right now, he wanted to find out how soft her lips really were.

'Brace yourself, Your Majesty,' he murmured, giving her one last chance to tell him no.

But she didn't, so he lowered his head slowly and pressed his mouth to hers.

She sucked in a breath, the giddy pulse beating double time against his thumb. He eased her into the kiss, slicking his tongue across the seam, gently, then more insistently, until she got the message. And opened for him. He pressed his advantage, tasting sweetness and spice… And all things nice. But as he probed, ready to go deeper, she jerked back.

He lifted his head, just as a knock sounded at the door.

She stared up at him—dazed.

Damn, but he could drown in those eyes, the mossy green sheened with heat and yearning, but also the panic he had sensed earlier.

Then she blinked and the shutters slammed down again. She took a step back.

He jammed his fists into his pockets to contain the urge to cup her cheeks, feel the heat against his palms—and take a heck of a lot more than just a kiss.

'Was that sufficient?' she asked.

*Not nearly.*

He eased a tight breath out of his lungs, and tried to remember this was all for show… And for his own amusement. Although his little joke had backfired, the heat now pulsing painfully in his gut.

'To be convincing?' she added, having regained her composure a lot faster than he had. Except… Her gaze wasn't meeting his again.

'I guess so,' he said.

She walked back around the desk, sat behind it, and steepled her fingers in front of her, but he could see her hands trembling and guessed she wasn't quite as composed as she was making out.

Well, good. Because neither was he. Somehow, though, she'd turned the tables on him and he didn't know how the hell she'd done it.

'Come in, Mel,' she called out when the knock sounded again. A young woman in a dark suit walked in pushing a silver carriage loaded with fancy china and set it up on the bureau at the back of the room.

'I hope you'll stay for coffee, Mr Lord,' the Queen said, polite as you please, which annoyed him more.

So, they were back to the formal. And that reserved shield of polite indifference. They were definitely going to have to work on that, once they were doing their loved-up act for the cameras. The thought of more kissing practice had adrenaline surging through his veins.

He thrust his fists further into his pockets as he watched Mel smile and leave the room. 'I need to head to the airport. But I'll be back in a couple of weeks with my surveyors,' he said. 'And the construction boss to do the initial surveys. If we can get the paperwork handled by then, let's arrange a time and place to make goo-goo eyes at each other and practise our lip action for the cameras.'

'Of… Of course,' she said, looking a little less sure of herself.

He smiled.

*My work here is done.*

'See you around, Belle,' he said, then strode out.

But as he headed back through the stateroom towards his waiting car, the feel of her mouth under his, and the vivid memory of that sweet sob of shocked arousal before her lips had softened and accepted his kiss, echoed uncomfortably in his groin.

And he couldn't help wondering what the hell he'd gotten himself into…

# CHAPTER FOUR

Back in Androvia TMW, checking out Ridge. Meet me @ 2 @ top & tip off press 4 pix.
T

ISABELLE REREAD THE message she had received on her private mobile phone yesterday, for about the ten thousandth time. She'd had to get Mel to translate it for her—because she had never received a text written in code before in her entire life. Luckily, her assistant was also her best friend and confidante, and knew about Isabelle's cunning plan to arrange a marriage with Travis Lord—and therefore release her from the strictures of her father's trust.

'How am I supposed to tip off the press?' Isabelle murmured. 'The only conversations I've ever had with them have been in press conferences. It's not as if I have the paparazzi on speed dial.'

Mel walked out of the dressing room with Isabelle's ski suit. 'Don't worry about that. I'll have a word with Hans in PR. He knows some local photographers. If he tells them you'll be skiing on the ridge this afternoon, they'll stake out Sariyelva,' she said, mentioning the picturesque town nestled at the bottom of the White Ridge gorge. 'Once they have photos of you with Lord, they'll be able to sell them to the highest bidder worldwide,' Mel added as she laid out the suit. 'It'll be a great boost to the local economy. Just make sure you end up there after your meet-up,' she finished with a quick grin.

Isabelle scowled. 'Easier said than done. I suspect directing Travis Lord to do anything is going to be like trying to herd a cat. A very big cat,' she added, barely able to contain a shudder at the thought of all those muscles.

She already knew he was going to look annoyingly magnificent in his skiwear. Because she'd seen photos of him modelling the Lord Culture brand. She tugged on her thermal undergarments. The silk felt like sandpaper against her oversensitive skin.

When exactly was her bizarre reaction to him going to end? She pursed her lips, aware of the tingling sensations that had tormented her for two weeks. She'd even had dreams about his kiss. His *stunt* kiss.

'Just remember, you're a queen, he's a commoner,' Mel said, giving her a confident smile. 'Dazzle him with your authority.'

'Believe me, Travis Lord is not a man who can be dazzled by anyone's authority but his own,' she said. And certainly not by someone with as little experience as she had of men. 'I got the definite impression he was more disdainful of my position than dazzled by it.'

'Then kiss him—and dazzle him with that instead.'

'What?' Isabelle swallowed heavily, the buzz on her lips joined by the hum at her core, which had plagued her at night, too.

'Do I need to kiss him?' *Again.* 'Won't being seen with him be enough?' She didn't want another fortnight of disturbed sleep, thank you very much. It was just over two months until Christmas—which meant her schedule was packed with official engagements already, because Androvia, with its array of Christmas markets and winter activities, was a luxury tourist destination for the festive season. One of her responsibilities as Androvia's sovereign was to promote that to the best of her ability.

Mel laughed, counting the reasons on her fingers. 'Firstly, you want to give the photographers an exclusive they can sell, and, believe me, a clandestine kiss will fit that brief perfectly, especially as you've never been caught kissing a man on camera.'

'Perhaps because I've never kissed any man on or off camera before I met Mr Lord,' Isabelle protested, then winced, realising how gauche that sounded.

No wonder her one stunt kiss with Travis Lord had had a far greater impact on her than it should. She was a complete novice. And how sad was that for a woman in her early twenties? But after acceding to the throne as an eight-year-old, she had not been afforded the romantic opportunities other girls took for granted.

Home-schooled in the palace until she was eighteen, she had then been enrolled in a private all-female college in Switzerland. But while the other students had been able to enjoy the nightlife in Zurich, Isabelle had concentrated on her studies—and been accompanied at all times by her security personnel.

'My point exactly,' Mel said, unfazed by the revelation, because Mel knew exactly how inexperienced Isabelle was when it came to men. And kissing.

Despite their differences, she and Mel had become firm friends as ten-year-olds when Mel's mother had become the palace's head chef. But while Mel had learned how to flirt with boys at the local community college as a teenager, Isabelle had been busy learning the protocols of how to host a dinner party for two hundred VIPs, or address the UN assembly. In many ways, Isabelle had lived vicariously through Mel, because she'd had no romantic adventures of her own—which would be sad, if it weren't so pathetic.

'Secondly, you're meant to be in love with the guy, that means making out like you can't keep your hands—or your lips—off him,' Mel continued.

'It does?' Isabelle said, her throat tightening. And the hum in her abdomen becoming a definite throb.

'Of course.' Mel smiled. 'Don't look so worried, Issy. You said you liked kissing him.'

'Well, he's very accomplished at it.'

'Then, kissing him again shouldn't be a problem. He's agreed to go through with this farce,' Mel added, because she had never been one hundred per cent on board with Isabelle's plan, believing a fake marriage was going above and beyond the call of duty. But then Mel had never really understood Isabelle's devotion to her role as Androvia's queen. 'Let him take the lead,' she said easily. 'It sounds like he's more than capable. And given that he's such a good kisser...' Mel's blue eyes twinkled with mischief '... you should enjoy it. Plus, you *definitely* need more practice, if you're going to have any hope of pulling this off.'

Isabelle nodded. 'All exceptionally good points,' she said—but her panic did not downgrade much. She sighed and breathed through the anxiety.

She needed to view her relationship with Travis Lord as a transaction—pure and simple. Lord was getting the land he wanted for nothing and she would finally be able to grow Androvia's economy with a string of infrastructure projects.

But just because this would not be a real romance, or a real marriage, there was no reason not to use this opportunity to explore being a woman as well as a queen.

She had never even flirted with a man before now. And when would she get the chance to develop those skills on a man as accomplished as Lord? He'd been mocking her when he'd initiated their library kiss. She'd understood that—while she'd been analysing the kiss in minute detail at two in the morning. However embarrassing that was on one level, it also gave her an opportunity. Because if he was going to use her—and their fake marriage—for his own amusement, she need not feel guilty making the most of his kissing skills.

He had not been indifferent to the kiss, any more than she had. Even with her total lack of experience she'd seen the dark shadow of awareness, maybe even arousal, in his gaze.

And the thrill had been... Not insubstantial.

They had already agreed that physical intimacy would not be a part of their relationship, but public displays of affection were required. So, really, more practice would not go amiss.

As Mel helped her pull on the ski suit, Isabelle decided she would not worry about her physical response to Lord— when it was a basic biological urge—especially as she would be able to control the outcome, thanks to their deal.

As the cavalcade of security vehicles drove to the end of the mountain track, Isabelle spotted a single black SUV stopped on the ridge, the engine still running. Lord stood alone a few feet from the vehicle with a large snowboard under his arm. He looked suitably striking and intimidating in a bright red ski jacket and black ski pants fitted perfectly to his athletic build.

*Figures.*

He signalled to his driver, and the SUV reversed and drove past them as Lord himself kept his eye on her entourage approaching.

After her security team had checked the perimeter, she stepped into the pristine snow, the lightweight ski boots she preferred sinking into the icy blanket with a crisp crunch. She dragged in a heady lungful of the clean cold air. They were a good three and a half thousand metres above sea level here, which had to explain why she felt light-headed, while the throb of anticipation could only be the rare chance to spend an afternoon skiing.

One of her staff placed her skis in front of her. She dug her feet into the bindings and thanked the young man, before putting on her goggles and gloves while she waited for her guards to equip themselves.

Once the whole party was ready, she skied smoothly across the ridge towards Lord, who hadn't budged. Why was she not surprised he was making her come to him?

She reached his position, with two of her security team flanking her and two more trailing behind.

'Hello, Mr Lord,' she said, his expression unreadable behind a pair of designer sunglasses. He wore no hat, or goggles, his dark unruly hair ruffled by the slight breeze. She kept her gaze fixed on his face, and not on his physique in the striking outfit.

'Call me Travis, Belle,' he said, using the ridiculous nickname again. Before she had a chance to comment though, he directed his gaze over her shoulder. 'What's with the circus?'

'Excuse me?' she managed, before she realised he was referring to her security team. She had become so used to taking the guards with her wherever she went, she didn't really notice them any more, but she could see from his scowl he was not pleased.

'Your babysitters,' he clarified, with typical bluntness. 'Why do you need them in the middle of nowhere?'

'It's procedure,' she said stiffly, determined not to let him aggravate her straight away. 'And we won't be in the middle of nowhere once we arrive in Sariyelva,' she added, pointedly. 'Which is where we are supposed to end up so the local press can photograph us together.'

'Then tell them we'll meet them there,' he replied coolly.

At least he hadn't objected to their destination, she thought ruefully. 'I also need them on hand to protect me.'

'From what?'

'Threats against my safety,' she said, firmly.

Why was he being so difficult? Having the security detail with her had felt hideously restrictive when she was younger. For years, the constant shadow had made her feel both suffocated and self-conscious, her every move monitored and measured, but she had come to accept the intrusion as a requirement of her position over time. And he would have to do so now, as well.

'Are we talking assassins and kidnappers or bears and broken bones?' he asked.

She bristled. What exactly was he implying, that Androvia was the Wild West? Or that she couldn't ski as well as he could snowboard?

'We do not have any intelligence about bad actors in the region. The bears are hibernating at this time of year, and I'm not going to fall. I happen to have been skiing almost as long as I've been able to walk,' she announced, her irritation getting the better of her, despite her best intentions.

'Terrific,' he said, dropping the snowboard onto the ground. 'Then tell your minders to scram and we'll see them in Sariyelva.'

'I can't ski without them,' she said, her patience starting to fray. 'They need to know I'm safe at all times.'

'You *can*, you're their boss,' he said, giving her instructions as if *he* were *her* boss—the self-righteous bastard. 'I'll make sure you're safe on the ride down. And they can track your phone if they need to.'

'I'm not going to ask them to…' she began, but he cut off the protest, by placing his chilled hand on her cheek, his familiarity shocking her into silence.

'Belle, listen up. This is non-negotiable. The deal's off if you can't get rid of the audience for an afternoon. I'm not comfortable with them trailing us everywhere we go. And no way are we going to persuade anyone we're an item if we're never alone.'

She started, shocked not just by the demand, and the ultimatum, but the familiar touch. And the way it made her feel—as if she wanted to jump out of her skin and lean into his callused palm at one and the same time.

'I just… I'm not used to doing anything alone,' she said, then wished she hadn't, because it made her sound pathetic.

But instead of mocking her, he brushed her cheek with his thumb. The caress was slight, but had a predictably shocking effect, before he let her go to lift his sunglasses.

What she saw in his expression wasn't the disdain she had expected.

'You're not alone, you're with me. We're gonna need

privacy to figure stuff out. And the downhill will be a lot more fun without the guard dogs.'

She cleared her throat. *Fun.*

Her temper deflated.

Hadn't she once longed for the freedom to do exactly what he was suggesting?

She took a steadying breath to consider his request—without letting her annoyance at his high-handedness get in the way.

It was a glorious day, the afternoon sunlight making the snow glisten and sparkle, and the forested gorge was the perfect gradient for a fast and challenging descent. The aloneness, the stillness, the silence—only broken by the cry of a raptor hunting in the blue above them—were spellbinding, vibrating with the possibility of adventures she had been denied for so long.

*Would it really be so wrong to indulge yourself, just this once?*

She swung round to address the head of her security detail before she could overthink the impulse. 'Jensen. Could you and the team meet us at the trailhead near Sariyelva?'

'Are you sure, Your Majesty?' the man said, frowning.

'Yes, myself and Mr Lord are going to ski alone,' she added with an authority she didn't entirely feel—but which only made the thought of playing hooky for the afternoon more exhilarating. 'We should be there in two hours at the most. Give me the satellite phone,' she said, holding out her hand to take the device. 'If there's a problem, we'll contact you.'

The man looked past her towards Lord, not at all happy about the instruction. Lord simply raised an eyebrow, and she could almost hear him saying, in that deep, husky American accent: *Yeah, so what you gonna do about it, buddy?*

The silence stretched, the stand-off between the two men vibrating with tension… And annoying her. Why was Jensen confronting Lord when this was her decision to make?

But then her security chief nodded and handed her the phone. Capitulating to her or Lord she wasn't quite sure—but she would take it.

'We will be waiting to escort you into Sariyelva,' he said. 'If we don't hear from you in two hours, we will send out a search party.'

'Of course, and thank you, Jensen,' she said, the spurt of adrenaline becoming intoxicating at the thought of having the whole afternoon to herself.

Jensen and his men returned to their vehicles and drove away, leaving the two of them alone on the ridge.

Lord fixed his feet into the snowboard's bindings, then bent to tighten the straps, apparently so confident he would win this round, he wasn't even going to gloat over his victory.

Isabelle's irritation spiked. She dug her sticks into the snow, determined to take back control of their afternoon excursion.

'Race you to the bottom, Mr Lord. The last one there is a rotten egg,' she shouted over her shoulder as she launched herself off the crest, flying into the undriven snow like a missile fired from a starting pistol.

The adrenaline was like a drug as she slalomed down the slope at breakneck speed, her muscles singing, and heard him shout from behind her: 'You're on.'

*Who knew? Her Majesty has some serious moves—and a killer instinct to match.*

Travis grinned as his fake date for the afternoon shot down the steep slope, switching through the turns to carve tracks in the untouched snow ahead of him…

The old exhilaration pounded through his veins as he gained ground by taking the more direct route. Her lithe figure bent over her skis as she ramped up her stick action to increase her speed—aware of him catching her.

Strictly speaking, skis were a faster way to travel on snow than a board—because two long thin sticks of fibreglass were aerodynamically a more efficient form of transportation than the shorter board he was using. Plus, the rider could distribute their weight more efficiently.

But he had a few key advantages. He was bigger, more badass, and, however good she was, she was still an amateur who had never risked her neck to win a race…

His bad leg jarred as the board hit a rock under the snow. He rebalanced himself, then gritted his teeth and crouched lower to push harder.

She glanced over her shoulder—her face a picture of shock, then grim determination.

His grin widened, despite the pain in his kneecap, as he swept past her. He could ice the knee later. Much later.

The slope reached the tree line, the conifers too tightly packed for even him to risk racing any further, so he looped round and slammed into a stop.

'I win!' he shouted.

She skidded, spraying him with snow as she was forced to brake hard a couple of feet above him.

He tugged off his sunglasses and flicked off the film of ice. 'Guess you're the rotten egg, Belle.'

She yanked off her goggles. Then threw them into

the air and laughed, her delighted expression making his heart pound.

'I don't care, that was glorious!' she announced. 'It's been so long since I've been permitted to ski that fast.'

'Yeah, who was stopping you?' he asked, intrigued, not just by the joy in her eyes, but also the sense of fellowship. He knew what it was like to get back something you'd figured might be lost for ever. While he'd never be able to board at the level he had before the accident, being able to ride at all felt precious now, even with the price he was usually forced to pay afterwards if he pushed too hard… As he had today.

'No one…specifically.' She brushed her hair back from her face, releasing the long blonde locks from the updo— which hadn't survived the ride. 'I just have certain responsibilities, ever since my parents died.' She glanced away, her complexion reddening in the chilly air. When she met his gaze again, the unguarded look had been replaced by something pensive. And wary. Was she thinking about her folks? Or just embarrassed she had revealed so much to a stranger? Because, although he hardly knew her, he had already figured out Queen Isabelle was not an over-sharer.

'That must be a royal pain in the butt,' he said, thinking it was a damn shame she never got to cut loose. 'Always having to do what you're told.'

'Not at all,' she said, the swift denial and the stiff tone contradicted by the colour still making her cheeks glow. 'I welcome the responsibility.'

'Uh-huh,' he said, letting his scepticism show. She'd enjoyed the race, why not admit it? After all, there was no one here to punish her for not being queenly enough.

'I didn't know you could race like that… After your accident,' she said.

'The accident wasn't that bad.' He lied smoothly, not liking the flicker of sympathy in her eyes, or the abrupt change of subject. 'And I'd have had to be dead to stop boarding. Or to let an amateur beat me on the downhill,' he added. 'Although you gave me a decent run there for about a nanosecond.'

A frown formed on her forehead—and he congratulated himself on locating the killer competitor again, behind the responsible rule-follower.

'A nanosecond?' she scoffed. 'You only beat me by a whisker, you…you…'

'Spit it out, it'll do you good…' he coaxed, enjoying her indignation almost as much as the sight of all that gold hair, flowing around her heart-shaped face. She really was a looker, especially with her hair loose.

'Your attempts to provoke me won't work, Mr Lord,' she said, trying to regain the decorum she'd lost so comprehensively during their downhill.

But he'd glimpsed the reckless girl, and he wasn't about to let her shut that girl down again so easily.

'Oh, yeah?' he said, then scooped up a handful of snow, pressed it into a ball and lobbed it straight at her.

She ducked just before it hit her, but the shock on her face was worth the miss.

He laughed, while arming himself with another handful of snow.

'What are you doing, Mr Lord?' she declared, while working her boots out of her skis.

*Clever girl.*

He snapped his own boots free, then tossed the ball from

hand to hand. 'Declaring a snowball war,' he said as he stalked towards her. 'Fair warning, Belle, you call me Mr Lord again and you're gonna be in big trouble.'

Her brows launched up her forehead as she retreated.

'You wouldn't dare…' she gasped, but he could see exhilaration—alongside her astonishment.

'Wanna bet?'

'But I'm a queen,' she said, falling backwards as she scrambled to get away. 'I could have you arrested.'

'I'll take my chances…' He fired the snowball, just as she turned and ducked again.

It sailed over her head. She jumped up and let out a triumphant hoot. 'You missed me…'

The second ball hit her square in the neck, filling her mouth with snow.

She let out a shocked gasp.

He grinned as she raced to arm herself.

He continued to advance on her—scooping up snow as he went—his adrenaline pumping.

He didn't care how much she loved the responsibilities of being a queen, everyone deserved a chance to cut loose occasionally. And seeing the mask of perfection slip was almost as much fun as beating her on the downhill.

They followed each other around the snowy clearing, snowballs exploding off the trees as they ducked and dived and shouted trying to gain an advantage. She was quicker than him in the cumbersome boots and had one hell of a throwing arm. But he was persistent and more willing to take the hits—which kept coming.

She landed pretty much every shot—but he kept advancing, ignoring the ice sliding down his neck, his frozen fingers or the snow coating his hair.

Finally, he had her cornered. Realising she was trapped, and all out of ammunition, she turned to make her get-away—a second too late.

'Oh, no, you don't...' He charged, throwing himself at her. Wrapping his arms around her hips, he swung in mid-air to take the brunt of the fall. They crashed together into a drift, her shrieking and him laughing so hard he was surprised he didn't bust a rib.

He lifted over her, pinned her wrists above her head, then shook his hair, until the snow landed in her face.

'I win again,' he declared, but he was still chuckling, while she was huffing and puffing and wiggling furiously under him.

'You bastard!' she announced—finally getting out the insult she'd wanted to call him earlier... Good to know a snowball fight could demolish all those years of stellar breeding in five minutes flat.

'Belle, sweetheart, you're only just figuring this out now...' He laughed some more, enjoying the flush of outrage and the sheen of exhilaration in her eyes. Until she wriggled some more, and a surge of heat hit him.

She went still, they both did. Then her gaze dropped to his mouth, her lips opening. The soft sob she made was like a siren call to his senses.

The urge to capture those full lips again streaked through him—as intoxicating as it was ill-advised. But he'd never been a guy to ignore his instincts, or the clear invitation in a woman's eyes. So, he lowered his head, ready to feast on her this time—until she tensed and murmured, 'Mr Lord?'

He stopped, registering the shocked tone, and the panic in her eyes, alongside the awareness.

He let go of her wrists, rolled off her—and flopped onto his back.

*Dumb move, Lord.*

He stared at the snow-covered pines—and took several long deep breaths of the frigid air, while willing the heat to take a hike.

What the hell had he been thinking? Or rather not thinking.

'I'm sorry,' she murmured. 'I should not have let you provoke me into the snowball fight,' she added. 'It was totally inappropriate given our circumstances.'

Annoyance—mostly with himself—kicked him in the gut.

Why was she taking the blame when he was the one who had started the snowball fight…and initiated their almost kiss?

He let out a gruff chuckle—although he wasn't at all amused—to release the knot of tension, and the weird regret.

Playing rough and tumble with her had been a schoolboy error. But seeing her lose her usual reserve had also been fascinating—so he refused to beat himself up about it too much, even though the ache in his groin was even more pronounced than the one in his cruciate ligament now.

He turned his head, to find her lying beside him staring back, a confused, questioning look on her face.

'No apology required. The snowball fight was my idea, Belle,' he said gruffly, to get that straight at least.

He rolled away from her to stand, then leant down to offer her his hand.

'Come on. Let's head to Sariyelva,' he said.

She clasped his hand. Even through her glove, he could

imagine her skin so soft against his own as he tugged her onto her feet. *Terrific*.

She really was a petite little thing, he realised as he waited for her to brush the snow off her suit. When exactly had that become a major turn-on, too?

She lifted her hair, tied it into a knot, her expression closed, her movements cautious.

Shame, he thought. But he held back the urge to tell her how much he liked her hair down.

*She's not yours, Lord.*

'How long to the end of the trail from here?' he asked, to get his mind back on business.

'Sariyelva is nestled in the valley below. It shouldn't take us more than an hour to ski down to it through the forest.' She began to talk in that clipped rushed tone, which he had figured out from their first meeting was a sign of her nerves. He relaxed a bit. At least he wasn't the only one affected by their horseplay.

'The PR team have let some local reporters know I'll be there this afternoon with you—incognito.' She continued to talk too much.

'Cool, so I guess we better make sure we put on a convincing show. To clue your subjects in to our torrid love affair.'

Her gaze snapped to his, the blush firing across her cheeks.

Damn, but teasing her was irresistible—however dumb.

'Um…well, yes…' she murmured, her expression an engaging mix of panic and awareness.

She couldn't possibly be *that* sheltered—she'd been the monarch of a major Alpine country for most of her life. But even if the strange innocence that clung to her wasn't real, it wasn't helping him get the heat under control either…

He headed to the board, fitted his feet back into the bindings. 'It's your call, Belle,' he said, and tried to mean it.

Giving in to the temptation to kiss her would not be smart. But as they headed through the forest trails towards their rendezvous with her security team and the local paparazzi the urge to get his mouth on hers again resolutely refused to take a hike, along with the desire to tempt the reckless girl back out of hiding.

# CHAPTER FIVE

'BY THE WAY, Mr Lord, I'd like to thank you for signing all the paperwork so promptly,' Isabelle announced as she stood beside Travis Lord, staring at the huddle of historic buildings below them that made up Sariyelva—the town's fairy lights already twinkling in the gathering dusk.

The journey here had taken them over an hour and during that time they'd barely exchanged a word. Perhaps because they were both mindful of the barriers that had been lowered far too readily with their race and the snowball fight. Barriers that she had been determined to rebuild.

But as much as she did not wish to test those barriers, Isabelle knew she couldn't remain silent any longer. There was too much they needed to discuss… Especially concerning the wedding ceremony itself. And its immediate aftermath.

Unfortunately, she had been unable to address these important details as they'd skied, and snowboarded down the trail, because she had been tongue-tied by the memory of him wrestling her to the ground. And the intent expression on his face as his gaze had shifted to her mouth. In that moment, while he'd held her down in the snow, she'd seen something intoxicating in his eyes—not just approval, but need. And for a second—a pregnant, endless, disturbing second—her heart had slowed from a giddy two-step to a heavy, one-two punch—and all her hopes and dreams had centred on the fierce desire to have him kiss her again.

*Utter madness, obviously.*

What had she been thinking? Cavorting with him like a teenager? Because, even after an hour, the memory of his big body pressing hers into the snow, his heavy breathing from their exertions visible in the frosty air, his gaze dark and serious, still felt like too much—and also not nearly enough.

He glanced at her, his lips quirking in the half-smile she found aggravating and captivating all at once.

'I thought I told you there would be trouble if you called me Mr Lord.'

'Sorry, I meant Travis, of course,' she said, flustered—again.

Her gaze strayed to his mouth, then jerked to his face, to find him watching her. Her cheeks burned.

*For goodness' sake, Issy, stop thinking about the kiss that never happened.*

'We have a lot to discuss,' she blurted out. 'Especially concerning the wedding ceremony. I think it best we marry as soon as possible—to facilitate the lease agreement.' She began to talk too fast, the words tumbling out of dry lips as she struggled to regain her composure. And keep her focus firmly on logistics and not the memory of his mouth lowering to hers.

'Obviously neither of us wants to have a full-blown royal wedding, especially as this is not a real marriage, and time is of the essence, but once I tell the Ruling Council about our engagement there will be expectations that we—'

'What expectations?' He interrupted her.

The scowl had returned. The one he'd worn on the ridge while asking—or rather demanding—she dismiss her body-guards. It had occurred to her several times in the past hour—as she had tried to understand her subsequent be-haviour—that giving into that request had been the rock on which her common sense had perished. Or rather, very nearly perished.

'As I'm Androvia's monarch,' she began, attempting to gather what was left of her wits, again, 'my wedding will have to be in the public eye.'

The scowl deepened. 'How public?'

'Public enough to convince the world ours is a real mar-riage.'

'Give me specifics,' he said. 'A ballpark figure for guest numbers, media imprints, time frames, et cetera.'

'I can't possibly give you those figures until I've spoken to my Privy Council and employed a team to do the plan-ning.' She scowled back. 'I just wanted to make you aware a royal wedding—however low-key—is a public event. We will also have to arrange a short honeymoon. But I've al-ready cleared my schedule to accommodate a wedding date on the twenty-first of December, if that is amenable. So, a few days off over the Christmas break during which we would remain in the palace should suffice to fulfil the hon-eymoon commitment.' She stopped abruptly, aware she was babbling again.

'That's a lot of extra stuff you're asking me to commit to,' he growled.

Really? Was it that much to ask? When he was getting land worth millions for a single dollar? 'As I said,' she began *again*, 'I will endeavour to ensure the time require-ments are not onerous for you.'

He stared at her for the longest time. 'Okay.'

Relief coursed through her—even though she wasn't sure why. If getting the most basic of commitments out of him was this hard, how would she ever make this work for an entire year?

But before she could point this out to him, he added, 'I can make the twenty-first work, just about, to relocate my base to Androvia for the resort project.'

'Fabulous,' she said, unable to keep the edge out of her voice.

'But I have a couple of conditions.'

'What conditions?'

'We make the honeymoon trip two weeks instead of a couple of days and we stay at my cabin in Colorado.'

'But... *What?*' she asked, or rather croaked. 'But that really isn't necessary,' she said. 'A working holiday in the palace on Christmas and Boxing Day will be more than sufficient. Plus, we will be expected to make some public appearances in the days immediately after the nuptials. And between Christmas and New Year.'

'No way. The wedding is public enough. Plus I always take a couple of weeks off over Christmas to recharge. And if I'm going to have to play nice for the wedding, not to mention spend a year in Androvia, I'm gonna need the break even more than usual.'

She could hear the surly tone, but also the steely determination.

Panic made her throat close. 'But I can't commit to that... It's...' *Too intimate? Too dangerous? Too exposing?* 'I can't possibly take two weeks away from my official duties in December, and at such short notice,' she said hastily, trying to come up with a viable excuse not to spend a fortnight with him—especially at Christmas.

She hated Christmas. It had always been a difficult time of year for her, even before her parents had died, and one she had never enjoyed. The thought of being forced to celebrate it with a man like him, who she suspected already had the ability to see too much, was untenable. 'And it makes no sense to leave the palace,' she continued, 'when it will create a security nightmare—'

'Stop panicking,' he cut in, making her brutally aware she had revealed too much already. 'I'll agree to ten days in total, to accommodate your schedule,' he said. 'And I'll get my people to liaise with Jensen about the security once we go public with the engagement,' he continued, as if it were already a done deal. 'But it shouldn't be a problem. My place is secluded and private with only one access road. And if we keep the location under wraps, it'll take at least ten days for anyone to find us there.'

*Secluded? Private?*

The thought only horrified her more. Keeping busy was the way she got through the season, the way she rode out the storm of memories—and the hollow ache of loneliness—that had dogged her at this time of year ever since she was a child.

'But I…' she began, desperately trying to come up with reasons not to agree to his request. 'That's really not—'

But he interrupted her again. 'Quit freaking out, Belle,' he said, sounding reasonable. Far *too* reasonable. But the determination—which she remembered from their stand-off over her security detail—told a very different story. 'Consider those ten days a chance to let off steam and figure out the logistics of this arrangement. We're not gonna have any time together before the marriage, so we're gonna need time after to get to know each other.'

'But I never take more than a few days off at Christmas…' she tried again, feeling her panic rising. 'I have too many commitments. And I—'

'Then you'll have to cancel them. Like I said, Christmas is the only chance I get to go boarding and chill. Plus, I'm gonna need some guaranteed downtime away from the media after the wedding circus you're insisting on.'

*Christmas? Downtime?* The idea horrified her.

'But there's going to be so much to do…' She trailed off as his expression remained implacable and unmoved.

'There's always so much to do. What are you so scared of?'

'I'm not scared,' she said, desperate to convince herself now, as well as him.

She made herself breathe. Letting Travis Lord know of her fears, of how vulnerable she felt at that time of year, would just expose her more… Especially as the prospect of spending ten days alone with him was already catapulting her so far outside her comfort zone she was practically on Mars.

'Then what's the big deal?' he said, still being Mr Far-Too-Reasonable. 'My place has enough space we won't bump into each other if we don't want to, and you're probably gonna need some downtime, too.'

*But I never take downtime.*

She swallowed the revealing remark.

How had he managed to box her into a corner again? As he had during their snowball fight? With no ammunition left.

*Blast the man, he's outmanoeuvred me again. This is getting to be a really annoying habit.*

'Okay, fine.' She sighed, knowing it was not at all fine. But continuing to freak out, as he had so indelicately put it, would just put her at more of a disadvantage.

*You are a queen, you can handle anything, including a ten-day Christmas break with Travis Lord.*

Perhaps it wouldn't be that bad? She would simply have to keep her wits about her while she was in his home. And, strictly speaking, this would still be a working Christmas. He certainly did not seem the sentimental sort, so surely he would not insist on any of the trappings of Christmas that she had always avoided. And she did *need* to get to know him better, if only to figure out how to stop him outmanoeuvring her so easily. Plus, if she was going to spend a year pretending to be intimate with him, she needed to become comfortable with spending time with him. She would consider this a baptism of fire. And anyway, they would not be alone—because she very much doubted he cooked and cleaned for himself.

'Cool,' he said. 'You won't regret it.'

*Unlikely, seeing as I already am.*

He glanced at the sun, which was about to dip below the horizon. 'Come on, we have a date with the paparazzi.' He stamped his feet back into the bindings of his snowboard. 'FYI, don't forget to look like you adore me as soon as we hit town, Belle.'

Her heart pounded against her ribcage—and pulsed between her thighs.

*Precisely!*

# CHAPTER SIX

'PERHAPS WE SHOULD be holding hands, Travis?'

Travis felt the inconvenient shot of lust at the tentative question from the woman beside him as they strolled through the sleepy Alpine town together and he tried to ignore the five guys flanking them and scanning the chocolate-box houses of Sariyelva like Rottweilers.

The heat sparked in his gut at the artless expression on her face.

He'd been edgy ever since their almost kiss earlier. But as the hot flush spread up her neck he couldn't resist a smile.

This deal was already a lot more complicated than he'd imagined it would be. He hadn't counted on their chemistry—which was looking more problematic by the second. But even so, he'd pushed for a Christmas break when she'd insisted on a public wedding.

Their 'honeymoon' would be his last chance for at least a year to visit the hideaway he'd built in the Colorado Rockies—and where he always headed over Christmas and New Year to de-stress.

He'd be damned if he was going to break that tradition to accommodate his fake wife, when he was already accommodating her enough.

'Holding hands is kind of lame, don't you think?' he said.

'What exactly do you suggest, then?' she asked, frowning.

'How about we try this,' he said, and slung his arm over her shoulder.

She let out a huff of surprise against his neck. And the heat spiked.

Yeah, their chemistry was definitely going to be a problem… But he only hugged her closer when her security chief gave him the stink eye again.

'Your Majesty?' Jensen asked, clearly not at all happy seeing Travis manhandle his queen.

*Tough.*

'Tell your guard dog to back off, Belle.' He nuzzled her ear, deciding to go for broke as he spotted the flicker of a camera lens in the distance. 'We're on candid camera already.'

She shuddered—which he felt all the way to his toes—but announced crisply, 'It's okay, Jensen. Mr Lord has my permission to hold me.'

'Now put your arm around my waist,' he instructed, because she was as stiff as a board beside him. Seriously, if he didn't know better, he'd think she'd never snuggled with a guy before.

She reached around his waist, her fingers curling into the fabric of his ski jacket—the gesture so awkward, it was almost sweet.

*Go figure.*

He tried to stroll with her under his arm, but her body was so rigid beside his she couldn't get into step with him.

'Relax, Belle,' he murmured. 'You adore me, remember.'

She huffed out a scoffing breath, but the teasing had the

desired effect and she finally began to soften enough not to fall on her face.

They headed into the main town square followed by their entourage, including the still scowling Jensen.

Dusk had fallen and fairy lights hung from the rafters of the wood-framed buildings, sparkling in the evening light. The place looked magical, like the set of a romantic movie, or a winter fairy tale. The locals stopped to stare and smile at them but kept a respectful distance. Spotting a coffee house in the corner of the square, he released her from the shoulder hug and grasped her hand to tug her towards it.

'Let's get a hot chocolate,' he said as inspiration struck. 'I'm parched.'

Isabelle's eyes widened. She was clearly taken aback by the suggestion.

He knew the plan had been to get photographed together and then split before they could cause too much commotion. But he wasn't ready to let her go just yet.

'I… Okay. But I'll need to check with Jensen,' she said.

He forced himself not to object. 'Go ahead.'

The presence of her security team had annoyed the hell out of him up on the ridge—and was one of the reasons why he'd nixed any official engagements straight after the wedding and pushed for the Colorado trip. Putting up with the constant scrutiny was going to be a major pain in the butt during his year in Androvia, which he hadn't really considered until now.

It took a good five minutes of negotiation for Jensen to agree to the detour on the condition they remained in sight.

'Of course,' Isabelle said. 'But could you find somewhere discreet to observe us?'

Jensen gave a curt nod and the team fanned out ahead

of them. Once they'd checked out the café, and alerted the proprietor, two of the team sat at a table on the far side of the porch while the others took up positions at vantage points around the square.

Isabelle turned to him. 'Okay?' she asked.

*Not really.*

He swallowed his frustration and squeezed her fingers. 'I guess.' Leading her up the porch steps, he asked the proprietor—who had rushed out to greet them—for a table for two.

'Yes, of course, *monsieur*,' he said, then bowed so low to Isabelle, Travis was surprised he didn't topple over. 'It is a great honour and privilege to have you frequenting our establishment, Your Majesty.'

Travis bristled some more. Isabelle might be their queen but she wasn't a supreme being—and the way people treated her like one was getting old fast.

The guy directed them to a table on the porch beneath the eaves, with enough bowing and profuse thanks to get on Travis's last nerve.

He was used to some media scrutiny, and occasionally to being spotted and asked for his autograph—especially back when he'd been a champion sportsman—but this was next level. He was going to need the ten days after the wedding just to figure out how to handle this kind of attention for a year. How the heck had she managed to deal with it for a lifetime?

Isabelle, though, seemed unfazed, the polite shield firmly back in place as she thanked the man graciously.

Travis ordered a couple of hot chocolates, fully loaded—even though he was jonesing for a beer.

Once the proprietor had left them alone, he lifted her

hand to tug off one of her gloves, then threaded his fingers through hers. The photographers were still shooting from across the square—but he knew the move wasn't entirely selfless when she shivered deliciously.

'That's gotta suck,' he said, keeping his voice low, so only she could hear.

'What has?' she asked.

He gauged her reaction, and realised she had no clue what he was talking about.

He had a vision of her as she had been as a young girl—taking on the responsibilities of a monarch when she was still grieving, still just a little kid. The weird pang of sympathy—and anger—on her behalf stabbed under his breastbone.

*Not your business, Lord. Not your problem.*

As far as he was concerned, monarchy was a load of hooey, a clever way to push tourist numbers and maintain the status quo. But he'd never given any thought to what it might be like for the people born into those roles. Was it a privilege or a curse?

A perplexed expression furrowed her brow and he had the sudden desire to make her forget they were on show.

He traced his thumb down the side of her face. Her vicious shudder had the heat curling in his groin—and the desire to distract and unsettle her became even more compelling.

Who cared if this was a business proposition? Didn't mean they couldn't give those parasites a show they'd remember.

He lowered his hand to rub his thumb across her knuckles.

'Don't you hate people treating you like a queen, instead of a woman?' he asked, attempting to focus on the conversation, while also focussing on that plump bottom lip—which had captivated him in the forest.

'Oh, that...' She released a breath, her relief obvious. 'You get used to it. I suppose.' The wistful sigh made him wonder if she was lying to him now, or to herself.

Their drinks arrived, and an unguarded smile brightened her features. 'I've never seen so much cream. Thank you, this looks delicious,' she said to the young server, who beamed then left them alone again.

She lifted the long-handled spoon beside the tall glass, scooped a marshmallow off the top and popped it in her mouth.

'You're doing it all wrong,' he murmured.

'I... I am?' she asked. The concerned furrow made him smile, her artlessness almost as appealing as how easy she was to tease.

'Yeah.' He lifted his own glass and took a sip, aware of the cream hitting his upper lip.

She gave a surprised chuckle when he lowered his glass. Then pulled a paper napkin from the dispenser.

'Here,' she said, reaching across to hand him the napkin, the stiff self-consciousness finally fading.

He snagged her wrist—and felt her stiffen right up again as awareness flared in her eyes.

'Not so fast, Belle,' he said, the devil in him ramping up as her pulse punched his thumb. 'Why don't you kiss it off?'

Her delicate brows shot up her forehead. And he saw her throat contract as she swallowed. 'I... *Really?*'

'Uh-huh. It'll make the perfect picture,' he said, as if this were still just for show... And had nothing to do with the heat that had been building all afternoon.

She turned, but he grasped her chin to prevent her from searching out the photographers.

'Pretend they're not there,' he said. 'And it's just the two of us, on a hot date. We want this to look convincing,' he said, smoothly, even though he felt the opposite of smooth right now—the desire in his gut already convincing enough.

She gave a slight nod. But uncertainty and self-consciousness still shadowed her expression—as if she really had no clue how to approach this.

'Take a sip of your own drink,' he directed, realising he was going to have to talk her through the process... Why did that only make the need more vicious? The desire more intense?

Surprise flickered in her eyes, but the awareness remained—rich and vivid—as she did what he told her. The lust in his gut twisted and pulsed.

What would it feel like to have this woman following his instructions in bed?

She placed the glass back on its saucer, her fingers trembling but her gaze direct. The white moustache on her top lip made him grin, even as the heat plunged deeper.

'Good girl,' he said, then tugged on her wrist to draw her closer. 'Come here.'

Again, she followed his instructions without question.

But as she leant across the table, that telltale sob issued from her lips. It was like a bullet to his gut, triggering a chain reaction.

And suddenly not one damn thing—certainly not the security team standing guard, not the photographers busy taking intrusive pictures, not even that uneasy feeling in his gut that was screaming at him this felt way too good to be fake—was going to stop him taking what she offered this time…

He slanted his mouth across hers, letting go of her wrist to cradle her cheeks, angle her head for better access, and capture that sob at last.

He licked and sucked and nipped—coaxing, encouraging, exploiting—until she opened for him on a heady breath, and let him in.

Her taste was even more intoxicating than the first time—warm rich chocolate, thick luxurious cream, and heady elemental desire.

He devoured her, exploring the recesses of her mouth. Until he had forgotten about everything but the hot sultry taste of her… And what he planned to feast on next.

Desire and longing barrelled through Isabelle's body, her mind dazed, her pulse thundering, as Travis Lord's lips claimed hers in a kiss that went from coaxing to carnal in a heartbeat.

She shivered, only vaguely aware of the table edge digging into her ribs, or his fingers caressing her scalp while he held her head. And took more.

Sensation vibrated from her breasts to the sweet spot between her thighs, and every pulse point in between. Her mind drifted into a sensual fog, dominated by the thrust of his tongue—and the desperate ache in her sex. The yearning to feel him there too, conquering her most intimate place in the same way as he was conquering her mouth, shot through her consciousness—wild, reckless, exciting, and absolutely terrifying.

She wrenched her mouth free, shocked by the direction of her thoughts, and how quickly they had roared out of control.

'Damn.' He groaned, then grinned at her—the smile knowing and arrogant.

Panic sprinted up her spine, doing nothing to obliterate the gush of need still making her sex ache.

He dropped his forehead to hers, his breathing as strained as hers, his strong hand massaging the tight muscles in her neck.

Sensation feathered her cheek, the scent of chocolate on his breath so rich and evocative she couldn't seem to make her mind engage.

'That should convince them,' he murmured, his thumb brushing the hammering pulse in her collarbone. She stiffened, the words throwing ice water over her flushed skin.

Of course, this kiss wasn't real for him, any more than the first one had been. It was all for the benefit of the photographers. She lifted her head, dislodging his hand, and blinked furiously, trying to control the brutal yearning and the cruel twist of humiliation.

His pupils had dilated to black, but other than that he was totally unmoved—as assured as always—while the heat he had incited still raced through her bloodstream, threatening to incinerate what was left of her common sense.

'Yes, I think that will be more than sufficient,' she managed around the boulder lodged in her throat.

Did he know? What his kiss had triggered? That the minute he had taken her mouth with that sense of entitlement and demand, she had been lost to the passion?

He captured her chin and turned her face to his, then wiped away what was left of the cream on her top lip with a napkin.

'You good?' he asked.

'Yes, thank you,' she said, although nothing could have been further from the truth.

Especially when his lips quirked. 'What are you thanking me for, Your Majesty?'

*For kissing me as if you meant it.*

The pathetic thought humiliated her even more.

'For making that so convincing,' she said, still trying to wrestle her wayward emotions back under control. 'I appreciate it,' she added, desperate to persuade herself this was still just a transaction.

But then he tilted his head to one side, his gaze roaming over her with the same fierce entitlement that had made his kiss feel so overwhelming.

'It wasn't exactly a hardship, Belle,' he said. His gaze dipped to her mouth, which began to tingle alarmingly— the memory of his conquest still playing havoc with her senses. 'That mouth is kind of irresistible.'

*It is?*

She sank her teeth into her bottom lip to stop herself from acknowledging the foolish feeling of validation at the compliment.

'I'm glad you think so,' she said. 'You happen to be a very accomplished kisser, so I guess that makes us even,' she added, trying to sound sophisticated and not devastated.

She had the awful suspicion she hadn't fooled him though, when he let out a gruff chuckle.

But the intense heat in his gaze didn't seem to have the cynical edge she had come to expect when he replied, 'Yeah, I guess it does.'

He was humouring her. They weren't even at all. Because sex was a game to him, while it could never be one to her. But still her pulse slowed when he stood and offered her his hand.

'Show's over,' he said, grasping her fingers. Sensation shot up her arm—because of course it did. 'We've given those vultures enough to run with for now.'

'Yes, of course.' She gulped down the spurt of regret—knowing that giving in to the impulse to spend more time with him would be even more dangerous than that ferocious, all-consuming kiss.

He dumped some of the local currency on the table.

'I can get my security to pay,' she offered.

His gaze flattened, the amusement gone.

'No, thanks, Your Majesty,' he said, the cynical edge back. 'When I take someone on a date, I pay.'

*Except this isn't a real date*, she wanted to protest.

But how could she, when it had felt far too real to her?

# CHAPTER SEVEN

*Two months later*

ISABELLE BREATHED OUT SLOWLY—but the constriction under her ribs from the corset she wore under antique ivory silk was nothing compared to the constriction in her throat as she observed the seven hundred carefully selected guests from her vantage point in the vestry.

Androvia's famous White Chapel was looking suitably stunning, its five-hundred-year-old eaves decorated with a thousand ivory and red Alpine roses, accented with edelweiss and local greenery, and artistically arranged by a team of fifty florists. The tall candles tied with velvet bows—which lit her route down the aisle—shimmered in the wintry light that shone through arched stained-glass windows and made the whole scene glow with a timeless beauty.

She stepped back to allow the hairdresser's assistants to finish fussing with her hair, while the stylist and her team made the final adjustments to her gown and the wedding planner briefed the six pageboys and bridesmaids who had been selected from local schools to carry her train and throw rose petals.

'You look beautiful, Your Majesty,' the stylist said in hushed tones. 'Mr Lord is a lucky man.'

*I'm not sure he would agree with you.*

Isabelle cut off the errant thought. 'Thank you, Maria.'

She took another constricted breath as she imagined seeing Travis Lord again, for the first time since their kiss in Sariyelva.

The correspondence between her government officials, the Ruling Council, the wedding planner and Travis's coterie of assistants and advisers and Lord Culture's management and PR teams had been fast and furious and at times exceedingly fraught ever since the pictures of their kiss had broken in the press, the morning after their fake date.

The media attention—when the engagement had been officially announced two days later—had been intense and intrusive ever since. Even though Travis had returned to the US that night and she had spent the past two months fulfilling as many of her official duties as was practicable, the whole world had continued to speculate feverishly about every aspect of the 'fairy-tale romance' between the 'bad-boy billionaire and the alpine queen'.

Given the media scrutiny, it had been decided they wouldn't release official engagement photos as any more meetings in person could only add to the furore. Not to mention distract from the intense planning necessary to arrange a major state occasion—however low-key—in a scant eight weeks.

The Ruling Council had been aghast at her haste, and her privy council had gone into a complete meltdown over the logistics, but they hadn't objected when she had insisted on a very short engagement. Each time she had repeated the lie though—that she was madly in love with Lord and could not wait to marry him—it had become harder and harder not to panic at the prospect of seeing him again.

Their marriage was a fraud, so why had her nerves only increased as their wedding day drew near?

Ironically, the only things that had alleviated the stress were the texts she had received on her private phone from Travis, himself, which had started when their engagement had been announced and continued every time he had an issue with the wedding protocols—which had turned out to be rather a lot.

Her heart bounced against her ribs as she recalled those unconventional texts—the man's demands and her increasingly forthright responses...

The truth was, she had begun to anticipate his messages—reaching for her phone first thing each morning to see if another had arrived—almost as often as she had panicked about her wayward response to his kiss, which was also far too frequent an occurrence.

She pulled her phone out from the gown's secret pocket—as the stylist continued to fuss—and scrolled through their latest exchange from four days ago, while struggling to even her breathing.

Travis: Tell Arne no way am I wearing a uniform when I'm not in the military. A monkey suit is bad enough.

Isabelle: I will tell Arne not to insist, as long as your monkey suit passes muster.

Travis: Don't u worry about my monkey suit.

The winking and laughing emojis that had accompanied the text had confused her when she had first read the message. Was monkey suit a euphemism of some sort that she was unaware of? She had puzzled for two agonising hours over how to respond appropriately, as she had done with so many of his texts. This time though, with her nerves already on edge, she had become so annoyed with herself she had opened the emoji keyboard for the first time in her life and dashed off one of a hand with a middle finger lifted. Of course, the second after she had pressed send, she had realised how utterly inappropriate her reply was—despite the increasing familiarity that had seeped into their conversations over the past weeks. But while she had still been frantically trying to figure out how to delete her reply, his response had appeared.

Travis: Expect payback for that on our honeymoon.

The thrill that had shot through her had been even more inappropriate—and disturbing—than the impulse to use a profane emoji in the first place.

And after four days, during which her anxiety had continued to build, she still hadn't been able to figure out where that urge had come from, or how to repress the thrill at the thought of seeing him again, which had only become more pronounced.

'Shall I take that, Your Majesty?'

Isabelle glanced up to find the wedding planner smiling at her politely.

'We don't want it going off while you're walking down the aisle,' the woman added.

'Of course.' Isabelle switched off the phone and handed it over, but the stab of loss and regret—as the planner tucked the phone into her pocket—only increased her anxiety.

Why had she become so excited by those silly communications over the past weeks? Checking incessantly every morning to find out if he'd sent another? Being secretly thrilled when she opened the app to find one of his disgruntled complaints waiting for her, no matter how contrary? Then procrastinating endlessly over her response.

In the last week, she'd even taken to scrolling through their past conversations, late at night, like a schoolgirl with a silly crush, instead of a queen negotiating with a business partner—albeit a somewhat unconventional one. She'd found his irreverent sense of humour and his dogged determination to ridicule Androvia's centuries-old traditions amusing, when she should have been appalled. She was Androvia's monarch, surely it was her job to respect and uphold those traditions, not joke about them?

With those thoughtless exchanges she had blurred the boundaries between them, exactly as she had during their snowball fight and while obsessing about their stunt kiss?

'Hey, Issy, are you okay? You look kind of spooked.'

Isabelle lifted her head to find Mel standing in front of her. Her best friend handed her the bridal bouquet, while looking beautifully poised and relaxed in her cream silk maid-of-honour gown. But Issy could see the concern in her eyes.

'Yes, yes, of course,' she managed, pasting on what she hoped was a competent smile. After all, she could hardly confide in Mel the reason for her latest panic attack—because she hadn't told anyone about her clandestine text conversations with Travis.

She could see she hadn't fooled Mel though when her friend frowned. 'It's not too late to call this whole thing off, you know, Issy,' she whispered gently.

Of course it was, but even if it weren't, Isabelle knew

she didn't want to call it off… She refused to examine the reasons why too closely.

'Really, I'm just tired,' she tried to reassure Mel, as well as herself. 'The stylist and the beauticians have been fussing for hours already, and I'm keen to get this over with now.'

The itinerary that had finally been agreed upon for the wedding day included events right up until midnight. But the thought of what would happen after that—when she and Travis were supposed to repair to her private apartments for their wedding night—had her anxiety, and the pulse of yearning that had refused to die for two solid months, spiking.

She ignored it.

*Not a real wedding, not a real wedding night. End of.*

Thank goodness her apartment in the palace had several bedrooms. And Travis had already agreed to the terms of their marriage. She might have blurred the lines a little over the past weeks—thanks to the wedding stress, and his innate ability to make her do stupid things, not to mention stunt-kiss her senseless—but she would never put her end goal in jeopardy.

*Never.*

'Okay, well, if you're sure,' Mel said, not looking convinced. 'By the way, Rene has just arrived. Late. And hungover,' she added, her voice edged with contempt.

Mel had never liked Androvia's neighbouring playboy prince. When they had been ten-year-old girls together in the palace, Issy's friend had often called out the teenage Rene for teasing both her and Isabelle whenever he came on an official visit accompanied by his father. But in recent years, her friend's contempt for the neighbouring monarch seemed to have intensified.

Isabelle felt a pang of sympathy for the man. 'I really wish Arne hadn't asked him to stand up for me,' she said. 'I hope he's not hurt.'

She'd been horrified when her chief courtier and the head of her household had informed her that, as a third cousin twice removed on her mother's side, Prince Rene was her nearest male relative—and therefore would be expected to walk her down the aisle.

Unfortunately, she'd been unable to come up with a viable excuse not to ask him.

'Hurt? How can he be hurt, when he doesn't have any emotions, other than narcissism, arrogance and lust?' Mel shot back.

'Because he asked for my hand himself, once,' Isabelle offered, her guilt mounting. Luckily no one but she and Rene and Mel knew about the proposal, but even so, this situation could not be more awkward.

'You were eighteen at the time, Issy. And you know as well as I do, he only asked for your hand because he was looking for a royal virgin to be his brood mare. Given the number of women he's dated since you turned him down, I think he got over your rejection pretty fast.'

'Then why does he seem upset now?' Isabelle asked, the guilt still weighing on her. Mel might dislike Rene, but Isabelle had started to believe he had been trapped by his circumstances and might never have been happy with the role assigned to him by fate—unlike her... From what she could remember of Rene's father, Sven Gaultiere, the previous Prince of Saltzaland, the man had been a cold, cynical and ruthless autocrat. Was it any surprise his son had become a reckless libertine as soon as he had acceded to the throne at eighteen? That said, after ten years, it probably was about time Rene settled into his duties.

'He's not upset, he's hungover,' Mel hissed.

The delicate strains of the violin solo shimmered on the air, introducing Pachelbel's 'Canon in D', played by the chapel's famous string quartet, and lifted the hairs on Isabelle's neck. And thoughts of Rene were superseded by a shocking rush of yearning.

Isabelle tensed as everyone took their places—and the knot of anticipation threatened to cut off her air supply.

But as she stepped into the chapel's nave with Mel and her pageboys and bridesmaids arranged behind her the knot tightened. And throbbed.

Rene appeared from the shadows, resplendent in a dress uniform, and gave a curt bow before offering her his arm. 'Your Majesty,' he said, with barely a hint of his usual sarcasm.

He was a strikingly handsome man—if you could ignore the brittle cynicism that never left his eyes—but as Isabelle placed her fingers on his arm, she noticed his complexion did look a little pale, his expression pained.

'Hello, brat,' he murmured to her maid of honour.

'Go to hell, Gaultiere,' Mel snapped under her breath, because she had never stood on ceremony with Rene.

'Could you two behave?' Isabelle whispered, but the familiar animosity had some of the tension in her gut easing. At least a little.

*You can do this, Issy. It was your idea and now all you have to do is see it through.*

The strings swelled accompanied by the chapel's antique organ as the canon built to a crescendo—along with Isabelle's rabbiting heartbeat.

'Ready?' Rene asked, with surprising thoughtfulness.

Isabelle nodded, unable to speak.

They headed down the aisle together, her heartbeat going into overdrive as she spotted the tall man standing alone at the altar, his broad shoulders, lean hips and long legs perfectly displayed in the expertly tailored morning suit.

The eyes of the congregation—made up of everyone from European royalty and heads of government to tech billionaires, supermodels and Hollywood stars—followed the bridal procession, the hush somehow pregnant with purpose, but Isabelle couldn't detach her gaze from the back of her groom's head, even as she struggled to keep the wave of panic and yearning under strict control.

Then he glanced over his shoulder—and their gazes collided.

Her breath became trapped in her lungs as she found herself marking each minute difference in his appearance since Sariyelva.

He'd had a haircut, she thought inanely, recalling those silky locks against her skin while they'd devoured each other in the café.

His gaze glided down her body, searing and intense— and with a sense of entitlement that made her panicked heartbeat plunge between her thighs.

Did he like what he saw? Why should it matter? When this whole circus was simply for the benefit of their onlookers?

His gaze landed back on her face as she reached him, potent and provocative. Her lips buzzed—almost as if she could feel his mouth branding hers again.

Rene presented her arm to Travis and murmured, 'Here you go, Lord, you lucky bastard.'

The Prince stepped back. And she forgot all about him as Travis folded her fingers over his arm and brought her to his side. Her constricted lungs filled with the clean, spicy scent of cedarwood and man. And suddenly she couldn't breathe. Had he got taller? How could he seem even more overwhelming now than he had that afternoon?

He adjusted the collar of his shirt, loosening the grey silk cravat at his neck.

'I hope to hell that dress is more comfortable than my monkey suit,' he murmured.

She smiled at his mocking tone—which reminded her of those irreverent texts—not easy given her breathing difficulties and the nerves that were now threatening to strangle her.

'You lose,' she whispered back. 'I'm wearing a corset.'

His gaze raked over her cleavage, which pressed against her décolletage. His eyes darkened and she wanted to bite off her tongue. Why had she said something so provocative? So flirtatious?

He lifted her hand to his lips—watching her as if she were the only person there—and pressed a kiss to her knuckles.

She jolted, the firm pressure like a lightning bolt to her already overwrought senses.

'You win this round, Belle,' he said.

But as the surge of awareness rioted through her body on a wave of need and panic she suspected she was not the winner of this round.

Because she suddenly felt like that reckless girl again, the girl she had glimpsed again in the forest clearing with him… The one who had once yearned to be loved and cherished, but who had ended up unable to control anything in her life, at all.

# CHAPTER EIGHT

*Eight hours later*

*IF I HAVE to listen to another damn speech, I'm gonna lose what's left of my ever-loving mind.*

Travis Lord tapped his foot under the banqueting table, in the four-centuries-old hall the size of a football field filled with hundreds of people, the vast majority of whom he didn't know from Adam, and tried to control the frustration, and the energy overload, that had been driving him nuts for hours.

He'd never been good at sitting still for long periods—even in high school he'd been thrown out of class more times than he could count because of the adrenaline that hurtled through his veins when he had to focus on any task for more than thirty minutes straight.

He'd trained himself to stay focussed for longer than that over the past decade—because being the CEO of a multinational brand meant attending a ton of really tedious meetings. Plus, he'd known getting through today's schedule was going to suck from the outset, but he'd thought he'd prepared—by working out for three hours in the palace's gym this morning before getting trussed up in this monkey suit.

What he hadn't factored in, though, and he should have,

was being close enough to touch his new bride for eight solid hours without a break. Having to breathe in that tantalising aroma of flowers and female musk, feeling her delicate shivers—every time he pressed his palm to the small of her back, or held her hand for the benefit of their audience—had been bad enough. But for the past two hours, he'd been less than five inches away from her—during ten never-ending courses of cordon bleu cuisine—forced to watch as she took delicate bites of the fancy food or judicious sips of the vintage bubbles, unable to forget exactly what it felt like to have those lips on him.

He stole another glance and took a swift hit to the gut, ramping up his frustration even more… But he couldn't seem to look away, even for his own sanity.

The embroidered silk gown emphasised every one of her subtle curves, while her blonde hair was piled on top of her head in an artful array of jewelled clips and combs that he'd been itching to pull out for hours. He stared again at the single curl that dangled down and caressed the graceful curve of her neck every time she moved. He imagined placing his lips, right there, to lick the spot where her delicate skin pulsed, then sucking it until she moaned. His gaze glided back to her cleavage, her full breasts plumped up against the neckline of her gown, and imagined the corset she'd mentioned at the altar, eight long hours ago, which he'd been obsessing about ever since.

He tore his gaze away and stared at the crowd of guests.

Lifting the spoon from the dessert he hadn't touched— because the last damn thing he needed right now was a sugar rush—he rapped it against the gold rim of his plate in a vain attempt to distract from the heat in his gut.

One thing was for sure, he should have made more of an effort to control this reaction before today.

Why hadn't he taken the edge off in the past two months as he'd planned?

He'd known their chemistry was going to be a major issue, ever since that kiss in Sariyelva.

The memory of her livewire reaction had consumed him ever since. Enough that he hadn't been able to face the thought of hooking up with any of his old dates since having his mouth on Isabelle—even though he was now staring down the barrel of twelve months of enforced celibacy.

And how exactly had he gotten suckered into their weird semi-sexting conversation in the past eight weeks too, which had somehow upped the ante even more?

He still didn't know what had possessed him to send that first text to her private number. But she'd replied. And he'd begun to prise open the box of polite reserve she wore like a shield to uncover the smart, witty, forthright girl beneath… He hadn't been able to resist pushing and poking at her for a whole lot more. Until she'd shot the bolt and sent him a middle-finger emoji.

The desire he'd been struggling to control ever since he'd turned to see her walking towards him this morning kicked him in the gut again.

He placed a hand on his own knee to stop the incessant foot tapping as the Androvian prime minister continued to drone on about 'the wonderful new union between our two countries'.

But then the words Isabelle had whispered to him at the altar shimmered across his consciousness.

*You lose. I'm wearing a corset.*

And the insistent foot tapping began again.

*Damn it, Lord. Time to make a break for it.*

He needed to get out of here. Before he got any more fixated on all the ways he wanted to seduce his fake wife on their non-wedding night.

Reaching under the table, he placed his hand on Isabelle's knee and squeezed. She jolted, and her head swung towards him. The shudder of awareness did nothing to control the pain in his groin… But the delicious blush sprinting across her features—which had only become more vivid as the endless day wore on—was some consolation.

At least he wasn't the only one suffering.

He leant close to whisper in her ear. 'I need to leave now, or I'm going to throttle your PM and ruin the wonderful new union between our two countries.'

'But the schedule is not finished…' she began—but he could feel her jolt of shock as he rode his hand up her thigh. 'There is still dancing.'

'No buts, Belle. And definitely no dancing,' he added.

'Why not?' she asked, her thigh trembling, even as her eyes widened.

Was she really that clueless about what her nearness was doing to him? Surely she couldn't be? But when she continued to stare at him, her full attention on him for the first time since they'd been at the altar, he decided there was no harm in being straight with her.

They were both adults after all. And while he'd made a deal and intended to stick to it, ever since *that* kiss, the thought of suggesting a compromise—so they could both work this chemistry out of their systems—was starting to make a lot more sense. They were due to be spending ten nights alone together in Colorado. If he'd been frustrated sitting next to her for eight hours, how the hell was he going to handle a week and a half?

'I can't dance, Belle,' he said, pressing his lips to her ear. Her delicate shudder fuelled his resolve to stop avoiding the obvious. 'Because I've been hard on and off ever since that damn corset comment.'

A hot blush scalded her cheeks, but he could also see the flash of panic in her eyes.

*Okay, what now?*

Why did she look so shocked? She'd kissed him back that day, and hadn't they been flirting—after a fashion—for eight weeks via text message?

'I see,' she said, biting into her bottom lip—the thought of which had been driving him wild for months, too. 'I'm sorry… I don't know why I mentioned that.'

'Hey.' He squeezed her thigh then let her go. 'Don't apologise.'

He'd thought they'd been on the same page. But maybe they hadn't been, because she still had that surprised look on her face.

'It's not that big a deal,' he said, even though it was getting bigger by the second. 'But I want to split now, before I explode.'

She signalled instantly to Arne, the stick-in-the-mud courtier who had been directing the schedule all evening.

The man hastened to her side and bent low. 'Your Majesty? How can I assist you?'

'Arne, myself and Mr Lord would like to repair to our private quarters now,' she said.

Hang on a minute… They were *both* leaving?

Her face had gone the same shade as the beets his mom

had once badgered him to eat. He'd hated them then, but he was liking them a lot more now.

'I'm afraid that's not possible, Your Majesty, the event schedule does not conclude until—' the guy began stiffly.

Travis's temper spiked. 'Forget it, Arne,' he interrupted. 'We're out of here.'

Arne went scarlet, but then bowed. 'Yes, certainly, Your Highness. I will make the necessary arrangements immediately.'

*Your Highness?*

He cringed, uncomfortable with the form of address all the staff had been using since the wedding.

Arne the stickler backed off—then began directing traffic to facilitate a speedy exit. It took less than ten to get the go-ahead, because Arne was nothing if not efficient.

Travis escorted Isabelle from the banqueting hall—through the throng of people giving them a standing ovation and sending them looks that suggested they knew exactly why they weren't hanging around.

But as they left the hall, Travis could feel her trembling under his guiding hand. Leaving him wondering again, what was going on?

Had the corset comment been a come-on or not?

Did she want him to strip it off her, as he'd been dreaming of doing all evening? Or did she want to stick to the original deal? She'd kissed him as though her life depended on it in Sariyelva, and their flirty text convo over the last couple of months had exposed more of that girl who intrigued the hell out of him. But she'd barely looked at him since they'd met again at the altar.

The staff finally left them as they reached the door to her private apartments in the palace's east wing.

'Alone at last,' he murmured as he shoved open the door, and she walked into the ornate salon ahead of him.

She didn't respond, didn't even look over her shoulder as she walked into the elaborately furnished space. She banded her arms around her waist, her stance rigid, then flinched as he shut the door.

Why did she look like a lamb being led to the slaughter...? Because it was making him feel like an overbearing jerk or, worse, the kind of guy he had always despised. Men like his old man, who seduced women for the hell of it.

He dumped his jacket on one of the overstuffed antique chairs, loosened his cravat—and decided to address the elephant in the room, which was now sitting on his chest.

'We need to talk, Belle.'

She swung round. 'About... About what?' she asked as their gazes locked for the first time since they'd declared their vows. Their *fake* vows—which didn't feel quite as fake as they should as she stood there in her wedding dress, trembling like a leaf, her expression a captivating mix of awareness and anxiety.

'About whether you want to change the terms of this agreement? Or not?' he asked.

The pulse in her neck beat double time. 'Which terms are you referring to?'

He yanked off the cravat, undid the top buttons of his dress shirt and frowned, not sure if she was playing games now, or if she was actually serious, because her expression had gone carefully blank.

He wanted her, and he was fairly sure she wanted him. But she was sending him a ton of mixed messages. Messages he needed to decipher before they went any further.

Because, unlike any other woman he'd ever dated, they

were going to be stuck together for a year, so he didn't want to screw this up right off the bat.

He sighed. Plain speaking it was, then.

'The no-sex terms,' he said bluntly. 'What else?'

'You… You wish to have sex with me?' Isabelle said, so shocked—and, God help her, excited—by the blunt statement, she didn't realise how gauche she sounded until his lips quirked.

Her grandmother's antique Louis XVI armoire creaked as he leant against it, then crossed his arms over that magnificent chest and let out a chuckle—which was so husky it scraped against all her most sensitive spots.

He didn't answer her for the longest time—making her wonder if he was trying to unnerve her.

'Yeah,' he finally replied. 'Correct me if I'm wrong, but I kind of thought we got that straight downstairs. Isn't that why you left with me?'

'No… I…' The denial choked off in her throat as he crossed his legs at the ankle—making the fabric of his trousers stretch over impressive thigh muscles—and drew her attention to the ridge in his pants.

*I've been hard on and off ever since that damn corset comment.*

She swallowed around the rock in her throat, which had also become wedged between her thighs. She forced her gaze back to his face. He was still watching her. Her nipples drew into tight peaks. Thank goodness, he couldn't see that reaction thanks to her corset, although…

*Stop thinking about the corset.*

'I just… I had to… I couldn't.' Her explanation got stuck behind the rock.

*For goodness' sake, Issy, spit it out.*

'I couldn't *not* leave with you. This is supposed to be our wedding night. We had to leave together, for appearances' sake…' she finished, which was mostly true, except—leaving with him had not been a hardship.

'Right.' His lips curved into a wry smile, as if he knew just how much she was lying to herself. 'Which brings us back to my original question…'

'I'm sorry, what was that?' she asked, because her grasp of the conversation had become tenuous at best.

'Do you want to go for a real wedding night to kick off this fake marriage in style?'

Ah yes… *That* question.

The rock wedged between her thighs grew to impossible proportions.

'Because I'm thinking we deserve some light relief,' he continued in that matter-of-fact tone, which made the rock pulse and glow. 'After the eight-hour show we've just had to put on—not to mention the two months of crap we had to deal with to get to this point—don't you?'

His gaze raked over her and the hot rock pounded.

She should say no. Encouraging a sexual relationship between them would be fraught with all sorts of problems. Problems she had considered insurmountable when they'd agreed to this marriage.

But even though she knew she should reject his suggestion, her tongue refused to cooperate. She was still struggling to give him an answer when Elsa, her lady's maid, burst into the salon.

'Your Majesty, would you like me to undress you now?' the woman asked as she crossed the room, having failed to spot Travis leaning against the armoire.

'Um...' Isabelle began, tongue-tied all over again.

'I don't think so.' Travis stepped in front of the maid, blocking her path. 'Undressing Belle is my job now.'

Isabelle felt a burst of excitement at the commanding tone, but right behind it was embarrassment. Especially when Elsa's mouth dropped open and she blushed.

'I'm so sorry, Your Highness,' Elsa said, addressing Travis, her tone horribly chastened.

Travis frowned at the maid. 'Yeah, don't call me that. Mr Lord will do just fine.'

She heard the impatient tone, and his contempt for the title bestowed on him by their marriage, and shame washed over her. Why was she allowing him to speak to her staff like that? She should never have allowed her duty to her throne and her subjects to be obscured by her foolish obsession with this man, who didn't respect either.

'It's okay, Elsa,' she began, determined to smooth over the awkwardness even though she needed Elsa's help to get out of this dress. But when the woman began backing out of the room, Isabelle had no choice but to let her leave. 'I'm sure His Highness and I can manage tonight,' she added, before Elsa darted out of the door.

Suddenly, they were alone again. The visceral yearning was still there, but the sensual fog that had built up over the past hours had lifted.

'Now where were we?' he said, thrusting his fingers through his hair.

At the exact same moment she said, 'That was uncalled for, frankly—'

'Frankly, I don't think so,' he shot back, interrupting her. 'You're entitled to some alone time.'

'That's not your call to make…' she began, annoyed the statement had made her anger soften.

*He doesn't care about you, Issy. He's just throwing his weight around.*

But before she could say more, he rolled up his sleeves—to reveal tanned forearms, covered in a supremely masculine dusting of dark hair that matched the hair peeking out from his open collar.

Isabelle blinked, her indignation momentarily derailed by the realisation she had never seen this much of him before. Him or any man for that matter.

'Stop changing the subject. You still haven't given me a straight answer,' he announced. 'Are we hooking up tonight or not?'

This time it was a lot easier to find a reply. 'You actually expect me to sleep with you now? After you were so rude to my staff and—'

'I guess that's a no, then,' he interrupted her tirade. Then he strode across the room and grabbed his jacket. 'Where am I sleeping? I need to crash.'

Temper sparked and tore at her self-control—its force as unfamiliar as the hot rock still pulsing between her thighs.

'The main guest bedroom is through there.' She threw out an arm to point. 'I believe your luggage is already there. We share a bathroom, so I would appreciate it if you could be prompt,' she added, wondering how on earth she was going to get out of her dress.

'I'm gonna need a while in the bathroom,' he said. 'So *you* be prompt. And let me know when you're done.' He slung the jacket over his shoulder. 'I'll see you tomorrow morning, for ten fun-filled days in Colorado. Not.'

He strolled out without another word.

She stared at the space he had vacated. Furious with herself now as well as him. Why had she behaved like such a ninny all day? Good grief, she'd even considered taking him up on his insulting offer. The last thing she needed was to allow him to demolish what was left of her self-control—simply because he had an itch he wanted to scratch.

She was still fuming when it occurred to her she had a far greater problem than her fake husband's temper tantrum as she began trying to dismantle the elaborate chignon. Within minutes it had become a tangled mass that would put a bird's nest to shame.

She wrestled with it, becoming increasingly frustrated and frantic—and only making the mess worse—when three sharp raps made her jump.

'Time's up, Your Majesty,' came the low voice through the door to his bedroom.

'I'm not finished,' she said with as much authority as she could muster, while feeling flustered and upset. This was his fault. He'd dismissed her maid and now he was trying to bully her out of her bathroom time.

'Tough. You've been in there over thirty minutes. It's my turn now.'

*What?* How could she possibly have been in here half an hour? Surely, he was exaggerating.

But as she stared at her hair in the mirror, the blonde bird's nest starting to list to one side, she was forced to admit defeat. She hadn't been able to locate any pins for a while and her scalp was starting to ache. But how was she going to sleep with it like this? Because she needed her sleep, to deal with this infuriating man in the morning.

'But I haven't even bathed yet,' she said, miserable now.

Why had she let Elsa leave? When she needed her? It would be humiliating to call her back.

And how had he brought her so low, after only one night?

'Why not?' he asked through the door, the tone of arrogant superiority almost as unjust as the snap of self-righteousness and impatience. 'What the hell have you been doing in there?'

Temper rose up to choke her, obliterating the misery until all she could see was her ruined hair through a red mist of fury.

She marched to the door, flicked the lock, and swung it open.

'You arrogant bastard,' she declared, not caring any more about the use of profanity. 'This!' She threw her hand up to indicate the mess on her head. 'This is what I've been doing.'

But then the red mist cleared, and shock followed, as she realised he was leaning against the door frame practically naked.

Where were his trousers, and his shoes?

And why did his bare chest, visible through his unbuttoned dress shirt, have to look so magnificent? Was that a tattoo on his left pectoral muscle? Whose name was that scrawled across his heart under a dusting of chest hair? Her gaze trailed down, tracking the tantalising line of hair bisecting ripped abdominal muscles, and hip flexors that made her mouth water, only to land on a pair of stretchy black boxer briefs. The waistband hung low on his lean waist, the legs stretched tight over roped thigh muscles while leaving virtually nothing to the imagination at his crotch.

She swallowed heavily, before she choked. If she had

thought that thick ridge was impressive before, it was making her abdomen turn into a lava flow now. Was he erect? Or just extremely well endowed?

'What the hell happened to your hair?'

The gruff question had her gaze shooting back to his face so fast she almost got whiplash. Horrified heat seared her collarbone.

'Y-y-you…' She cleared her throat as the lava flow rose up to incinerate her cheeks—and dry her throat to dust. 'You happened to it,' she managed, beyond grateful to discover he had been focussed on her hair and was unaware of her checking out the contents of his boxers.

His gaze dropped to her flaming face. 'Uh-huh? How exactly is the Leaning Tower of Hair my fault?'

The asinine comment had her anger surging back to cover her mortification. Especially when his gaze roamed over her cleavage again—with that arrogant entitlement that had derailed her common sense earlier in the evening.

Well, he wasn't going to derail it again, she told herself staunchly. Despite the continuing lava flow from stretchy-boxer-briefs-gate.

She was now fully focussed on her main priority—which involved making this marriage work for the duration of the year they had agreed upon, and not risking torpedoing it for the reckless pursuit of temporary pleasure, which was clearly his priority.

She would have to be the adult here, because it was becoming increasingly obvious Travis Lord had never had to think about anything but himself and the pursuit of his own gratification.

Her spine stiffened with self-righteousness. Unfortunately, even standing tall, it didn't do much to decrease his massive height advantage, especially when he levered himself off the door, and stared down at her from his full height.

She lifted her chin, so she could glare at him—and not his left pec.

'It's your fault because you were so rude and obnoxious to Elsa earlier, she was scared to stay in the same room with you,' she said, upset all over again at the way he had spoken to her maid. 'And I've never had to do this without her.'

To her utter astonishment though, instead of mocking her for being unable to handle dismantling her own chignon, flags of colour appeared on his tanned cheeks. 'Yeah, you're right, I screwed up,' he murmured. 'So I called her and apologised.'

'You… You *did*?' she asked, so surprised by the admission she wasn't sure she could believe him.

But when he began to speak, his contrition was unmistakable, and disarmed her temper completely.

'I lost my cool. I'm not great at being on show for eight hours straight,' he said, the weary tone forcing her to admit she might have misjudged him. After all, she was used to official events, and today had been extremely taxing even for her.

'But I behaved like a dick and there's no excuse for that,' he continued. 'Plus my mom would have given me hell if she'd ever heard me talk to the help like that…' He trailed off. The dark sincerity in his gaze—and the mention of his mother, who Isabelle recalled had been a cleaner—made her heart slow and guilt prickle at the back of her throat.

She *had* misjudged him.

She had assumed he was one of those rich, entitled men who treated the people who worked for them with contempt, and she had disliked him intensely for it—on very little evidence. Which forced her to question her own motivations.

She could see now, she had *wanted* to judge him because over the last two months—during all those silly texts—she had found his blunt sense of humour so enjoyable, his irreverence so exhilarating and the way he saw her—as a woman and not a queen—impossibly exciting. And it had scared her. Because wanting him to kiss her again, to make love to her even, wasn't nearly as terrifying as acknowledging how much she had enjoyed his attention and approval.

It would be pathetic if it weren't so cowardly.

'I apologised to Arne the Stickler as well,' he said. 'Cos I was kind of a dick to him, too.'

'Thank you, I appreciate that,' she said, humbled by his honesty, and his willingness to admit his mistake not just to her staff but also to her.

He shrugged. 'You're welcome, Your Majesty,' he said with the wry humour that she found incredibly beguiling. As well as annoying.

He stared at the bird's nest on her head again. 'How about I take a crack at it?'

The sharp tug under her breastbone at the bold request was complicated by the heat sinking deep into her abdomen.

'Seems the least I can do after scaring off your maid.'

'I'm not sure that's a good idea,' she managed, far too aware of his state of undress and the slow thunder of her heartbeat.

Admitting how much she had come to enjoy certain aspects of his character only made him more dangerous to her peace of mind… And her flagging boundaries.

'You got a better idea?' he said. 'Cos it's close to midnight now, so hauling Elsa out of bed to do it is only going to make us both look like dicks.'

She huffed out a laugh, despite the rising tension. Why did she find the familiar way he spoke to her so appealing?

She dismissed the sentimental thought. Or tried to. And pressed her palm against the mass of hair, hopelessly aware of his focussed stare as he awaited her answer...

'It's okay, I should probably just sleep on it and let Elsa deal with it in the morning. It's a fairly major job and you're probably tired too,' she tried to reason.

'I'm not *that* tired,' he said, the sensual smile having a disturbing effect on her already erratic heartbeat. He captured her wrist—his touch as bold as it was sure—and drew her hand down. 'Seems like a job I ought to learn, just in case,' he added, his thumb rubbing casually against the pulse throbbing wildly in her wrist. 'Even as your fake husband you never know when I might need the experience.' The slow sensual smile spread. 'Plus, I've been wanting to demolish that hairdo for hours.'

'I... *Really?*' she said as her sex clenched alarmingly.

'Yeah. I should probably tell you,' he said, lifting her hand and opening her fist as he continued to speak in that lazy, husky tone. 'I've acquired a major hair fetish in the last couple months.'

'You... You have?' she said, inanely, but unable to think clearly.

'Uh-huh.' He pressed a kiss into the centre of her palm.

She jolted as sensation arrowed into her sex. She should object, should tug her hand free, but she appeared to be unable to do anything but inhale the enticing cedarwood scent that clung to him.

'Kind of perverted, I know, but I think we should work

with it.' Letting go of her hand, he placed his palm on her waist and directed her back into the bathroom.

Stopping in front of the large marble vanity, he placed his hands on her shoulders and turned her towards the mirror. He stood behind her, his broad shoulders somehow filling the large bathroom.

'So where do I start?' he asked, his tone casual, but the fierce purpose in his gaze as it met hers in the glass staggering her.

She directed her gaze to the rigid tangle of curls and clips and pins—trying to focus on the question, and the task at hand… And not the sight of him—so large and overwhelming behind her.

'If you could get the rest of the pins out, that would be a big help,' she murmured, feeling both hopelessly self-conscious, but also strangely exhilarated.

'Right, here goes. Tell me if it hurts, okay?'

She nodded, watching as he spent some time assessing the damage, then located a pin at her crown. He wiggled it then dragged it free, with infinite patience. Sensation sparked across her scalp, waking up nerve-endings that had been deadened hours ago.

His gaze met hers as he threw the pin on the vanity. 'One down,' he said. 'Only ten thousand to go.'

She chuckled, releasing a little of the tension in her stomach.

'Hey, don't laugh, I take my work seriously.'

She smiled, trying not to fall for his charm… Or get too fixated on the muscular torso so close to her back.

True to his word he worked diligently, watching her reaction intently as he located and pulled out each pin, each clip and comb. She stood as still as she could under his care, but it became increasingly difficult with each slow brush of his fingertips, each gentle tug, the silence as he concentrated on freeing her hair only making the task seem more intimate—and arousing.

By the time he had wriggled the final clip loose, her entire scalp had become a riot of sensation, her heartbeat thundering in her chest and echoing in her sex.

How had he made her head an erogenous zone?

He thrust strong fingers into her hair and the heavy mass cascaded onto her shoulders. A moan escaped her as he kneaded her scalp, massaging away the soreness.

'Better?' he asked as he dropped his hands to her shoulders.

Their gazes collided in the mirror.

'Yes, thank you,' she murmured, aware of his nearness, knowing how much she had enjoyed his ministrations. 'I should probably go to bed now.'

She went to step away from him, but he held her in place.

'Hold up,' he said. His hands skimmed down her bare arms to land on her waist. 'How about I help you with the dress?' he murmured, resting his chin on the top of her head.

The question sounded innocent, but the wicked light in his eyes as he awaited her answer was anything but.

The throbbing in her sex became unbearable.

'And the corset?' he added, with no pretence at all of innocence now. 'Because I've been dreaming of getting you out of that all day.'

The husky comment reverberated through her torso.

Would it be so wrong? To admit how much she wanted to feel those strong hands on her again? A part of her knew this was leading somewhere she had already decided they could not go.

But her previous cowardice came back to taunt her now. The hot weight in her sex impossible to ignore. And all she could do was nod.

# CHAPTER NINE

HUNGER TORE THROUGH Travis as Isabelle lowered her chin in the barest hint of a nod.

She was beyond beautiful, the cascade of curls like a golden cloud, her eyes dark with the desire she'd denied earlier.

*Progress.*

She'd never looked more like a queen in that moment—regal and proud. But also somehow fragile and untouched, the wary light in her eyes making her seem vulnerable.

The realisation he was going to have to work to earn her trust only captivated him more.

He inhaled her intoxicating fragrance—wild flowers and sin—then gathered the heavy locks, feeling her delicious shiver in response, and swept them over her shoulder.

He studied the fastenings of her gown. The tiny hooks were a problem, his hands weren't exactly made for delicate work, but he'd managed to deal with her hair without hurting her. He just needed to take it slow.

Locating the hook at her nape, he released it—the hunger surging as she shuddered. He worked his way down her back, freeing her from the garment, as each delicious quiver ricocheted through her body and into his.

Did she know how responsive she was to him?

By the time he reached her waist, the gown was gaping open to reveal the corset. He eased the ornate silk off her shoulders and she released a deep breath as the fabric pooled at her feet.

Damn, but her cleavage was like a work of art, her slender curves displayed in nothing but the cream silk corset, and some lacy panties.

'Thank you,' she said again, in that studiously polite tone, which only made her livewire responses to him more of a turn-on.

'Corset next?' he murmured, shifting back so she didn't become aware of the growing bulge in his shorts.

Again, she nodded. Triggering another surge of desire.

He needed to pace himself again so he took a moment to stare out of the bathroom window and slow his breathing. Snow drifted down in thick flakes from the canopy of stars in the night sky, blanketing the gorge below.

Mostly in control again, he assessed the corset's intricate tapes, rubbing his thumb across the reddened skin where the panels had dug into her back.

She bucked against the slight touch.

'Why did you need this thing anyway?' he asked.

'The stylist and the designer felt it would enhance my figure,' she said.

'Like it needs enhancing,' he scoffed.

The flush on her face flared, and he wondered again if she knew how gorgeous she was.

He went to work on the corset. But her vicious shivers as he released each tape only turbo-charged the heat that had been building between them for hours, days, months even…

Peeling off the stiff silk contraption at last, he placed his mouth between her shoulder blades and kissed the dewy skin. A soft moan broke from her lips.

Desire flared as the corset landed on the floor and he took in the sight of all that flushed deliciously pink flesh in nothing but a pair of minuscule lace panties and silk stockings held up by a suspender belt. She had clasped her arms over her bare breasts. But her shyness was as captivating as the arousal darkening her green eyes to black.

'Don't cover yourself, Belle,' he groaned. 'You're beautiful.'

He could see her surprise and pleasure at the compliment—which made no sense. Surely he couldn't be the first guy to tell her that?

The streak of jealousy—and possessiveness—at the thought of all those other guys made even less sense. They might be married, but she wasn't his.

Even so, he skimmed his thumb across her nape, delighted when her eyes flared with need.

Her arms remained folded over her breasts, but they weren't hiding much.

He stroked her bare shoulders, causing more of those delicious shivers. Circling her waist, he flattened his palms against her belly, just above the lace of her panties, to draw her against him.

'I want to kiss you again, Belle,' he murmured against her neck, determined to make it a question, even though the hunger was crucifying him.

'Where?' she asked—in that puzzled, polite way she had that he was beginning to realise masked so much passion.

His lips quirked. How could she be so hot and yet so adorable?

'Anywhere you'll let me,' he replied.

Her eyes glazed with arousal, but her teeth dug into her lip, the panic resurfacing. Grasping her shoulders, he turned her to face him—before she could get out the no he suspected might be coming.

'How about we start with this mouth?' he said, lifting her lips to his.

She blinked, then nodded.

*Thank the Lord.*

Isabelle's breath guttered out as Travis's lips captured hers.

But unlike the kiss she had obsessed about for weeks, this kiss wasn't coaxing or careful, it was demanding and forceful. A groan she couldn't control reverberated through her as she opened her mouth to welcome him in. Vicious sensation centred in her sex as his tongue thrust deep.

The pleasure spread like wildfire as he wrapped his arms around her to bring her flush against him. She could feel the thrust of his erection against her belly. Hard and long, and more than a little overwhelming even through his shorts. She writhed against the thick ridge, suddenly desperate to relieve the aching pain emanating from her core.

His head rose suddenly, and he tore his mouth from hers.

'I'm sorry,' she mumbled.

His lips curved in a wry smile, which had her wariness resurfacing. Could he see what he did to her?

'What for?' he asked, his gravelly voice scraping the many sensitive parts he had exploited so easily.

*Because I don't know how to do this.*

The words reverberated in her mind, too revealing to be said aloud.

'I'm still not sure this is a good idea,' she muttered.

He nodded. But the demand on his face remained as he cradled her cheek and dragged his thumb across her lips.

'If you want to tell me where you like to be touched, we could see if I can change your mind,' he said, the purpose in his gaze as intoxicating as the renewed throbbing in her sex.

Again, she should say no—she had no idea where she liked to be touched.

But her control was already in tatters, the aching desire consuming her, and another nod became inevitable when he skimmed his thumb under her bare breast—and shocking sensation arrowed down to her core.

He turned her around to face the mirror again. 'How about we start there?' he said, nuzzling the skin under her earlobe as he took her wrists to gently release the arms she had shielding her breasts.

Her harsh intake of breath echoed around the room as he cupped the heavy orbs.

'Good?' he asked as he circled the throbbing peaks while kissing the pulse in her neck.

She groaned. 'Yes.'

He let out a raw chuckle, but continued to caress her, toying with the responsive peaks as she leaned against him, her legs becoming boneless.

'So where next, Belle?' he asked, the husky tone making her body quake anew.

Her eyes fluttered open, and she met his molten gaze in the glass. That he was letting her set the pace, dictate his moves, felt empowering somehow—and spurred the reckless excitement.

How could this be wrong? When it felt so right?

'Just… Anywhere…' she managed, her voice thick with the yearning she could no longer disguise.

'Good choice,' he said.

His hands left her breasts to wrap around her body, holding her against him, making her aware of his need as well as her own.

She gasped, the surge of pleasure so immense she could no longer resist it, or him.

Fireworks burst in the night sky outside to mark the end of their wedding day.

'We missed the fireworks,' she murmured, inanely.

His gaze roamed over her—the coloured lights reflected in his eyes. 'No, we didn't.'

He wasn't wrong, she realised, because the thunder and pop from outside were nothing compared to the fire sparking across her nerve-endings as he held her close while his hands stroked and caressed, her breasts, her waist, her hips...

Her chest heaved as she stared at their reflection—her so small and needy, him so tall and commanding. He lifted her arm, draped it over his neck. She clung onto him, her breasts thrust out, the air trapped in her lungs as anticipation fired through her. Long strong fingers traced across her ribs, circling her belly button and finally delving into her panties, to locate the swollen folds of her sex.

'You're so wet for me, Belle,' he growled, sending a fierce wave of validation and approval through her molten flesh.

She moaned, her body a mass of sensation, the guttural sound both plea and prayer as he skimmed over her centre at last—the bundle of nerves begging for his touch.

Her legs weakened, her knees trembling, her thighs tensing and releasing as he circled and delved, forcing her to focus on that one raw secret spot as the pleasure built, and twisted, and burned.

'Please… I…' She couldn't talk, couldn't really say what it was she wanted. She'd never felt so exposed or so needy before, her senses heightened beyond what she could bear.

'I've got you, Belle, just relax.'

She tried to do as he asked as the tension gripped her body.

Then he eased one thick finger—with aching slowness—into her. She bucked, shocked by the intrusion, which triggered a bolt of pleasure so immense her desperation increased.

Then his thumb touched the very heart of her. The violent pleasure centred and crested—fierce and raw and unstoppable—shooting her over the edge, the vicious coil releasing in a rush.

She cried out as he worked her through the staggering sensations. She clung to his neck, bucking against his hand, as she rode that unending, unendurable wave of bliss to her limits and beyond.

The waves of orgasm weakened at last. Her whole body shook as he finally released her from the decadent torture. The glittering afterglow gave way to brutal reality as he clasped her waist and murmured against her neck.

'Ready for round two?'

She opened her eyes to find him watching her intently, his gaze dark with yearning. The long column of flesh thrust against her back as his palm moved to cup her backside.

She lurched away from the possessive touch. 'I… We can't.'

'No?' The fog of desire cleared a little. 'Why not?' Her

heart lurched in her chest as he bracketed her hips, the thick ridge cradled against her bottom. 'It's just sex.'

*Except it's not just sex to me.*

She turned, folding shaky arms back over her breasts—which were still tender from his ministrations.

Why had she let it go this far?

She wanted to believe theirs was nothing more than a strong physical connection—as he did—and perhaps the culmination of denying this aspect of her life for far too long. But her heart continued to do somersaults in her chest, and she knew she felt something for him, something she had never felt for another man, or she would never have let him dismantle her defences so thoroughly.

'I... I need to go to bed,' she said, frantic now, as well as scared. 'We have a long day tomorrow.'

One dark eyebrow hiked up his forehead. 'For real?'

'I'm sorry.' She eased past him, the fear rioting now, the feel of those strong fingers on her, inside her, still humming in her sex. 'I can't...'

She glanced down, aware of the thick erection straining against the front of his shorts, the outline making the throbbing in her sex worse.

'I'm not on any birth control...' she lied, grasping at a way to extricate herself with some degree of dignity. And poise. And conceal from him how utterly he'd overwhelmed her.

'I've got condoms,' he offered.

'But I can't risk...' she began.

'It's okay, Belle, we can always take a rain check,' he said, the passion clearing from his eyes to be replaced by—well, nothing. She couldn't tell if he was angry with her or not. 'This isn't a transaction,' he murmured, his expression shuttered and unreadable.

Was he angry? Could he sense her distress?

'Thank you, for being so understanding,' she said, in a desperate attempt to distance herself again. But what else could she do? She'd let him see too much.

He'd given her something incredible, something she hadn't really believed existed until this moment. But beneath the woman he had awakened was that little girl who could be hurt far too easily—if she let herself want too much.

She needed time to rebuild her defences. And to close down the aching vulnerability in her heart, which he would never understand.

'Right,' he said, the slight edge in his voice making her feel ashamed once again of her cowardice.

She dashed from the bathroom and locked the connecting door.

It took her hours to finally fall asleep, though, her body still humming from his caresses—as she listened to him showering and imagined him naked and aroused.

By the time she finally fell into a fitful sleep, she had examined and discarded every possible outcome of her foolish decision to become intimate with her fake husband...

And every one of them was a disaster, starting with how on earth she was going to survive ten nights in his home in Colorado with her dignity and her sense of self intact. Because he had a power over her now that wasn't equal, or equitable. And she had already committed much more to this relationship than she could possibly afford to lose.

# CHAPTER TEN

'YOUR MAJESTY, LOOK this way! Can we see your smile? Are you looking forward to your first Christmas as a married woman?'

'Travis, what's it like to be a member of European royalty?'

'How is your first day of married life going, Your Majesty?'

Travis wrapped his arm around Isabelle's waist, tugging her closer, as the reporters and photographers fired questions, and the barrage of camera flashes blinded them both. They were supposed to be putting on a show here, for the world's media. A show he hadn't wanted any part of and wanted even less part of after the way last night had ended. Because touching her now—after watching her lose herself in his arms, then close herself off—was torture.

His frustration built, though, when she stiffened against him.

He tightened his hold on her. 'Relax,' he whispered in her ear as they stood together on the tarmac at the palace's private airfield, his company jet fuelled and ready to take them away from this circus.

Last night had knocked him sideways. He'd never experienced foreplay like it before. She'd been so vibrant and responsive to his touch, despite the weird innocence that clung to her.

For a moment, as she'd writhed and groaned, her body flushed with pleasure, her inhibitions gone, he'd felt as if he'd achieved something rare and special—which was sentimental crap, of course, but, even so, his ego had taken a hit when he'd heard the door lock click.

He'd had to turn the shower temperature down to frigid—and take himself in hand like a teenager, which had been humiliating. But it wasn't sexual frustration that had made it impossible for him to sleep afterwards.

He hadn't lied to her. As far as he was concerned, sex was never a transaction. It was always a woman's prerogative to say no. And he guessed the birth control thing was an issue—he certainly didn't want to add any more complications to this relationship when it was already complicated enough. But he'd seen the lie in her eyes when she'd offered up that excuse. And the panic and regret as soon as the afterglow had faded. Which had forced him to ask the question, why had she freaked out?

Because the hollow ache when she'd run out on him had reminded him of when he was a twelve-year-old kid, at his first junior snowboarding championship, and his old man had showed up with his 'real sons' and stood in the crowd to cheer for them, instead of Travis.

That would be the needy kid he'd buried a long time ago.

He didn't need anyone's praise or approval any more, especially not from the woman standing next to him—who wasn't even his real wife. So how had she made him feel like that dumb kid again?

'Travis, can you tell us why you two left the festivities

so early? And missed the fireworks? Was that planned? Or was it a spontaneous decision?'

Travis zeroed in on the young female reporter at the front of the pack who had shouted out the intrusive question. And was grinning at him now with deliberate innuendo.

Isabelle stiffened, but of course she didn't respond. Her dignified silence, though, and the memory of exactly what they had been doing when those fireworks had gone off had the last of his patience with this crap snapping like a dry twig.

He'd been advised by the press secretary not to respond to the reporters—that they wouldn't expect answers to their questions as it was all part of the protocol that the Queen didn't react.

But no way was he letting that pass.

'Why do you think we left early?' he said. 'We're newly-weds. How about you take a wild guess…?'

He heard Isabelle gasp, just before the media horde exploded into a cacophony of sound—each shouted question cruder and more provocative than the last.

The palace press secretary looked as if he were going to have an aneurysm. The expressions on the faces of the members of Isabelle's court and the representatives of the privy council—who had been assembled to see them off—had gone varying shades of shocked and appalled. While the palace guards had to use their decorative rifles to restrain the surging tide of tabloid hacks sensing an exclusive.

Isabelle went deathly still beside him—her cheeks stained a vivid scarlet, her emerald eyes glassy with shock.

*To hell with this.*

He grasped her hand. 'We're out of here.'

She didn't object, didn't utter a sound, probably because

she couldn't without making even more of a scene. But somehow her refusal to react only infuriated him more.

He didn't break stride as he marched across the tarmac with her hand gripped firmly in his, then led her up the steps into the waiting plane.

The steward closed the plane door behind them, shutting out the media circus. But as he led Belle into the jet's lounge, he could sense her disapproval, even as the regal mask—which had slipped spectacularly last night—remained firmly in place.

The volatile emotions hit critical mass and the hollow ache in his gut widened, just as it had on that day so long ago, when he'd aced every race, broken a ton of records taking stupid risks to impress a man who had looked right through him as if he didn't exist.

'Mr Lord, we're cleared for take-off whenever you're ready,' the pilot said, greeting them in the gangway.

'Great. We're ready now,' Travis replied. 'Let's get the hell out of here.'

The pilot nodded and headed to the cockpit.

'We'll strap ourselves in, Bill,' he said to the steward. 'Give us some privacy.'

'Absolutely, sir.' If the guy was surprised, he didn't show it. 'Just let me know if you want any refreshments once we reach our cruising altitude,' he finished before disappearing into the service pantry.

Travis walked through to the lounge, so on edge now he was surprised steam wasn't coming out of his ears. Isabelle had taken one of the leather armchairs and fastened her belt. Her face was still hot with embarrassment, but her expression remained impassive as she stared out of the window.

The tension tightened like a vice around his ribs.

He took the seat opposite her. The plane's engines rumbled to life, drowning out the furore outside.

He held his tongue as the jet taxied down the runway, waiting for her to give him hell for the crude comment, which was probably slapped all over the Internet already.

But Isabelle remained calm and unmoved, her hands folded in her lap, the only sign she even had a pulse the staggered rise and fall of her breasts beneath the tailored silk blouse—those would be the breasts he'd had in his hands the night before and discovered were supremely sensitive.

When the jet reached its cruising altitude—and the pilot informed them over the public address system of their eleven-hour flight time to Denver International—she still hadn't said a damn word. She hadn't even made eye contact.

Was she giving him the silent treatment?

*To hell with that.*

Leaning forward, he grasped her chin and directed her gaze to his.

'If you've got something to say to me, Belle, you best spit it out.'

She blinked, the mask of indifference collapsing to be replaced by something he liked even less... And recognised from the previous evening... Panic, and regret.

'I apologise. For last night. I should not have let things become so...intimate...' Isabelle murmured, both mortally embarrassed and out of her depth in the face of his anger—while also feeling like the worst kind of fraud. 'It was wrong to leave you unsatisfied.'

She'd sensed Travis's frustration, the impatience bristling under his skin, ever since she had met him in the chauffeur-driven car taking them both to the airstrip half an hour ago for the photo call before their flight. She had wanted to say something, *anything*, to defuse the tension and make amends for her selfishness, as she suspected it was not the done thing to enjoy a man's touch with the fervour she had enjoyed his, and then leave him visibly erect without offering him some relief.

But what could she say? When she knew not one thing about the etiquette of sexual relationships. So, she had remained silent.

She had paid for her cowardice though. Because having to stand so close to him during the photoshoot, while trying not to react to the heavy weight of his palm resting possessively on her waist, and the brush of his breath against her ear when he told her to relax—exactly as he had done the night before—had been excruciating.

He let go of her chin and cursed.

She flinched. Had she said the wrong thing? He didn't look pleased by her apology. If anything he looked even more frustrated. And appalled.

'Don't do that polite reserved crap with me, it drives me nuts. And don't apologise for last night. What the hell does that even mean?' He lifted his fingers to do sarcastic air quotes. '"It was wrong to leave you unsatisfied."'

She looked away from him again, her face on fire. 'It means I had an orgasm and you didn't,' she said, as calmly as she could while her hands were shaking. 'And I suspect that sexual frustration—and more specifically anger with my selfishness last night—is the reason you were unable to control your temper with that reporter,' she added, determined to acknowledge her part in this fiasco. 'Which is why I felt an apology was appropriate.'

He swore again, the word low with fury now. 'Exactly how much of a jackass do you think I am?'

'I don't know,' she snapped, her own patience starting to evaporate.

She was trying to do the right thing here. But she'd had a virtually sleepless night. And while she had no doubt at all she was partially responsible for this morning's outburst, there was a limit to how much blame she was prepared to take.

'Although so far you haven't surprised me,' she added, her voice clipped.

How was last night's fiasco and his difficult behaviour this morning all her fault? He was a grown man. And he was the one who had pushed to reset the terms of their agreement as soon as they had been alone together. Yes, she had been a willing participant in what had transpired—far too willing—but shouldn't he take some of the responsibility for this disaster, too?

He collapsed back into his chair and yelled another profanity at the ceiling—the anger making his chest flex under his shirt. The sight sent an inconvenient shot of awareness through her tired body—because the memory of exactly what all those muscles looked like, flexing in unison as he worked her into a frenzy, was now apparently tattooed on her frontal lobe.

*Fabulous!*

'Wow, you're really a piece of work, aren't you?' he said, his gaze fixed on her again, his dark eyes flinty with temper. 'How do you do it?'

'How do I do what?'

'Pull off the "ice queen" act like that.' He leant forward,

resting tanned forearms on his knees. 'When we both know there's enough passion inside you to set fire to Alaska.'

'It's not an act,' she said. Disturbed by the way he was staring at her now, with the same intensity that had terrified her the night before, as if he could see past all her defences, all the emotions she had learned to control, to find the insecure, needy girl beneath.

He laughed, the sound raw and brittle. 'Yeah, it is. Don't forget I've seen you when you're aching for my touch. Smelt your need when you're clambering for release. And there's nothing cold about you then, is there?' He leant back, his gaze searing in its contempt. 'You know, it would be pretty funny that you think I'm good enough to pretend to marry, but not good enough to touch you—if it weren't so damn insulting.'

Shock reverberated through her at the accusations she didn't understand.

*Superior? Not good enough?*

Her own temper died, consumed by confusion and regret.

Clearly, she had insulted him, without intending to. The thought seemed incongruous—given the man's ego up to now had appeared stronger and more resilient than the White Ridge itself. But when he turned away, she noticed the muscle clenching in his jaw and the dark flags of colour on his cheeks—and it occurred to her she might not be the only one who had allowed themselves to get carried away last night.

Strangely, the thought calmed her rampaging pulse and her own feelings of inadequacy.

She hadn't meant to insult him, certainly did not believe herself to be superior to him. But the fact he had not been completely unmoved by their intimacy made her feel a little less insecure, a little less powerless.

She swallowed, struggling to contain the inexplicable spurt of exhilaration at the thought she was not the only one who had been overwhelmed.

But how could she convince him her decision to leave so abruptly had nothing to do with her opinion of him and everything to do with her own inexperience? Without creating an even bigger minefield for them to tiptoe through in the days ahead?

'You said it was just sex,' she said at last.

His head whipped round, skewering her with a look that could immolate lead. 'So what?'

But this time, she wasn't fooled by that furious glare.

'I assumed that to mean you were not emotionally engaged in the physical intimacy we shared last night. But how can that be so if I hurt your feelings by leaving you unsatisfied?'

*Okay? What now?*

Travis stared at the woman in front of him, totally speechless for the first time in his life. And not sure now whether to be insulted, or angry... Or simply stunned.

He wanted to hang onto his temper, but it was impossible in the face of that curious expression that seemed as confused as it was forthright.

Hell, not only did he not know what to feel, he didn't even know what to think. Her careful analysis of last night both vaguely insulting and yet brutally honest at one and the same time.

One minute she'd been accusing him of being a class-A jerk who figured she owed him sex just because he'd given her an orgasm. And the next… Had she just accused him of being a drama queen as well as a jerk?

'I wasn't hurt,' he managed at last. 'That's just dumb. Believe me, I know how to handle rejection.' Even if he hadn't had to handle it in a long time, and certainly not in the bedroom before now… He had always respected boundaries when it came to sex—simply by never getting too invested in the outcome. Sex was fun, sex was recreational, it wasn't about emotional engagement for him and it never had been. Because that would make him a chump as well as a jerk.

But even as the denial echoed in his head, he was forced to admit no other woman had ever made him feel like he had as a kid again.

Surely that was just because she was a queen though, and their whole situation was more complicated than any relationship he'd ever had… And he hadn't even slept with her, yet.

'I see,' she said, in that infuriating way she had that made it sound as if she doubted he was being honest with her, or with himself.

'Listen, I don't get emotionally engaged when it comes to sex. Or relationships for that matter. And I never look for validation and approval from other people, because my old man taught me that was a mug's game when I was twelve years old,' he blurted out, determined to convince himself now, as well as her.

This relationship was no different from all the others he'd had over the years. Maybe their circumstances were a lot weirder. And her status had bothered him more than he'd thought—exposing an inferiority complex he hadn't even known he had until last night—plus the no-sex rule had added a challenge that he had found impossible to resist once their chemistry had become obvious... But that was it.

The sharp light in her eyes softened though, the curiosity turning to compassion.

'I thought you didn't know your father's identity,' she said, and he realised he'd said too much. *Way* too much. Because he'd just let slip a piece of information he'd worked hard to keep hidden. Not because he gave a damn what people thought of his origins, but because he'd never wanted to answer any questions about someone who meant nothing to him and had chosen not to be a part of his life. Plus, he hadn't wanted anyone looking at him the way she was looking at him right now—as if that bastard or his absence had had any impact on him.

Sure, not having a father had been tough at times when he was a kid, because his mom had been forced to work like a dog to keep them clothed and fed. But never having anything given to him on a silver platter had been a blessing in disguise, because it had made him that much more determined to win at all costs and on his own terms.

'I always knew who he was,' he said, because denying the truth now would just make it look as if he cared. 'My mom cleaned his place in Aspen for years.'

He shrugged, uncomfortable now, because she was still looking at him as if any of this mattered, when it never had, not to him anyhow.

'I think she had some dumb notion that if he knew about me, he'd want to be my dad. Because she was a romantic, who always believed the best in people, even him. And it was easier to kid herself he had loved her once—than face the reality that he'd taken advantage of a seventeen-year-old virgin who had a summer job cleaning his vacation home, while his wife and kids were out of town.'

He stared out of the window, the bitter taste in his mouth when he spoke about his old man annoying him. It was kind of lowering to realise that thinking about his mom's misguided attempts to rewrite the narrative of his parents' relationship could still make him mad.

'As far as he was concerned,' he added. 'I was a mistake he'd made that he didn't want to acknowledge. That upset her, but it was fine by me.'

'He sounds like a selfish and unpleasant man,' Isabelle said.

He let out a hollow laugh. 'Yeah, probably, I never met him,' he lied easily enough, because he'd given her too much information already.

She frowned. 'But if you never met him, how did he teach you about rejection when you were only twelve?'

*For the love of Mike! Why hadn't he kept his mouth shut?*

'It's a long story,' he growled.

'We have eleven hours,' she countered.

'It's a long *boring* story…'

*Which is none of your business*, he wanted to add. But didn't, because he was the dumbass who had made it her business and it sounded way too defensive.

'And I'm shattered,' he added, unclipping his belt.

'I understand,' she said. 'Royal duties are often more taxing than they look.'

'You're telling me,' he said, ignoring the prickle of unease that she was treating him with kid gloves now—as if he were some kind of hothead who couldn't keep it together under pressure.

But then he'd created that rod for his own back, by behaving like a jerk this morning—not just to the press, but also to her.

He'd accused her of judging him, when what he'd really been doing was judging himself—just as he had as a kid. No wonder he'd gotten all bent out of shape about nothing.

He thrust his fingers through his hair as he stood up, the pressure of the last twenty-four hours taking a toll.

He'd never been a guy to overthink anything, especially not his own emotions, but then he'd also never had to spend eight hours straight pretending to be in love with the whole world watching, while wearing a monkey suit and not being able to touch what he was already supposed to have.

*Note to self: marriage in name only totally sucks when you have the hots for your fake wife.*

He still didn't know why Isabelle had run off like that, why she hadn't wanted the quick stress fix that great sex could provide. Because one thing last night had proved was that she had the hots for him too.

But he had ten days in Colorado to figure out if there was a way they could make their chemistry work as a stress-relief valve without having it blow up in both their faces.

He'd also been pretty arrogant thinking the duties of monarchy were nothing. He could see that now. After less than twenty-four hours of living in the full glare of that spotlight he'd somehow managed to dredge up stuff from his childhood that he'd gotten over years ago.

He had to give her some credit for holding it together this morning when he hadn't. He was also pretty curious now about how she did that, while also being so artless and unworldly. Maybe it was just an act, but he wasn't as convinced about that any more.

'I'm gonna head to one of the bedrooms at the back and

crash,' he said. Then, because she was still looking at him like a stick of dynamite that might explode at any second, the devil got the better of him again. 'If you want to finish what we started last night, you're welcome to join me.'

Her face flushed a deep shade of pink—and her eyebrows rose. 'I... I don't think so,' she sputtered.

He grinned at her reaction. Good to know he could still unsettle her—because she sure as hell unsettled him.

'Lady's choice, Your Majesty.' He gave her a mocking bow, then headed to the bedroom. Alone.

One thing was for sure, he needed to get some shut-eye if he was going to stop himself from behaving like a dumbass again.

But as he showered, the thought of *actually* finishing what they had started had a predictable effect, and it occurred to him he needed to find a way to handle this hunger, if he was going to get what he wanted out of this deal—without crippling himself in the process.

*'I understand.'*

Isabelle stared after Travis as he strolled to the back of the plane, his teasing offer of finishing what they had started only making her feel more insecure and confused... And hopelessly turned on.

Why on earth had she said she understood him, when she didn't understand the man at all? Admittedly, her knowledge of men and relationships was extremely limited, but Travis Lord was already turning out to be a great deal more complex than she had assumed.

The revelations about his father had shocked her, but also saddened her—the curt, clipped tone when he talked about that relationship, or rather the lack of it, so unlike the relaxed, confident, and frankly shallow man she had believed him to be.

Because she had seen the strength of feeling even as he had boasted about his lack of emotional engagement and heard the suppressed rage in his voice, even as he had pretended his father's rejection had meant nothing.

How could that be the case? Surely no one could be treated with such casual cruelty by their own flesh and blood and come out of it unscathed?

But what had moved her even more was the sense of connection.

After all, she had suffered a similar loss in her childhood too, when her parents had died so suddenly. At the time, the one thing that had helped her recover from that loss was the knowledge they had died together, and that they had loved her very much—even if they had been unable to show it in demonstrative ways.

How did you survive the loss of a parent, though, when their absence in your life had been a choice, not an accident? Had Travis survived it by persuading himself he couldn't be hurt by it, even though he clearly had been?

Whatever the answer, it was clear a fascinatingly complex and passionate man lay beneath the veneer of relaxed charm and devil-may-care confidence. A man she needed to get to know better.

Surely if she could understand him, it would enhance the time they spent together over the next year. It would also help to ease him into the role of consort, and help her better manage the charade they were forced to play, which was clearly going to be more difficult for both of them than either one of them had assumed.

That said, she also knew she needed to be careful. Because while Travis Lord presented an intriguing emotional puzzle, he also had an aura about him—a latent, potent, sexual energy—which she found disturbingly attractive.

How could she be sure she wouldn't freak out again, and make matters even more difficult between them? Or worse, give in to this chemistry only to become overwhelmed by feelings he had made it clear would not be reciprocated?

She yawned as the young steward popped his head around the lounge's doorway.

'Would you like me to serve lunch now, Your Majesty?' he asked. Then peered around the lounge area. 'Is Mr Lord in the restroom?'

Isabelle found her cheeks burning again. How did she explain Travis had repaired to his bedroom, without her? Would the young man think it odd? Given that they were newly-weds? And what if he had heard their argument? Of course, she had to trust Travis's staff, like her own, knew how to be discreet. But it would be necessary over the next ten days to learn how to create the illusion of intimacy for a wider audience—and contain any more emotional outbursts.

'Um… No,' she murmured. 'Thank you. I think we're good for now.'

She frowned. Having spent her whole life knowing exactly what to say at any given time or do in any given circumstance, she had no idea what was the done thing in an intimate relationship with a man, let alone a marriage.

Apparently, if she was going to teach Travis how to assume the responsibilities of royalty over the next ten days, they would have to teach each other how to look like a couple in love. Even though it was obvious he had no more aptitude for that than she did.

As she made her excuses to the steward and headed to the *other* bedroom at the back of the plane, it occurred to her the tangled web she was currently weaving might very well end up strangling her... Especially given that the fascinating man she'd chosen to weave it with had also proved to be impulsive, headstrong, dominating, far too hot and completely unpredictable.

*Bother.*

# CHAPTER ELEVEN

ISABELLE'S BREATH CAUGHT when she glimpsed the huge steel and glass house as the helicopter flew over the forested gorge, before landing on a heliport on the far side of the ridge.

The vivid blue sky cast a clean, clear light over the Rocky Mountain range as far as the eye could see, spanning a staggering three thousand miles—south to New Mexico and north all the way to British Columbia. While the rock formations lacked the dramatic peaks and sharp descents of Androvia's younger Alpine range, there was something about the rugged, breathtaking terrain that made the land here seem wilder and more untamed.

Isabelle wrapped the thick down coat that she'd donned when they'd landed in Denver International around herself to climb down the helicopter's steps while Travis finished the flight checks with his co-pilot. She had hardly spoken with him since she'd woken on the jet to find him working on his laptop in the lounge, looking relaxed and far too handsome. Her grand plans to discuss all the things they should work on while they were in Colorado had hastily been put on hold as another bout of inappropriate yearning had assailed her.

Travis and the pilot began loading their luggage onto a

two-seater quad bike parked next to the heliport once the chopper's blades had stopped.

*How odd... Where are the house's staff?*

'Hey, grab that bag, Belle,' Travis shouted at her.

She lifted the small suitcase that contained her cosmetics and toiletries. And joined him at the quad.

'Sling it in the back and hop in,' he said.

She felt the surge of affection at the casual way he spoke to her. Then felt foolish for her giddy reaction. Surely, he spoke to everyone in the same way? Exactly how sheltered was she?

She thanked the pilot, who had finished loading the bags—which appeared to be all hers apart from a large rucksack—and climbed into the quad.

'Thanks, Chad,' Travis said, slapping the pilot on the back. 'We'll see you on the first for the pick-up. I'll check in with Megan if we need anything, but otherwise have a great Christmas.'

Isabelle tensed. She'd conveniently forgotten about the upcoming festive season—thanks to the pressures of the wedding and the wedding night. She forced herself not to panic.

She had a plan to refocus their working relationship over the next ten days.

All she needed to do was find the right time to suggest it.

The pilot waved goodbye, promising not to lift off until they were at the house.

After jumping into the quad, Travis drove through a grove of aspens laden with snow. The track opened out onto the valley ridge. Isabelle's breathing clogged again as his mountain home appeared. The striking multi-level structure was much larger than she had expected, and as breath-taking as the stunning panoramic view across the Rockies.

He'd called the place a cabin, so she'd envisioned something cosy and quaint made of wood. She certainly had not expected anything this modern—or this imposing. The steel and glass edifice was several storeys high and built into the ridge-line with terraces on two levels that ran the length of the house. A seventy-five-foot lap pool encased in glass hung over the cliff on the lower level. Steam rose from the water, which was open to the elements.

'You swim outdoors? At this time of year?' she asked.

He braked the quad in front of a four-car garage. 'Yeah, the water's heated to twenty degrees, so I don't freeze to death. Swimming is a good way to iron out the kinks after a day's boarding, or a workout in the gym here if the weather's not cooperating.' He slung his arm across the steering wheel, his gaze roaming over her—and sending her pulse into overdrive. 'I've always had a surplus of energy. I need to find ways to work it off during the day, or I'm ready to crawl out of my own skin by nightfall.'

'I… I see,' she stuttered.

He smiled, that slow sensual smile that had heat curling in her abdomen and made her feel as if she were about to crawl out of her own skin, too. Even though she had *never* had a problem with hyperactivity.

'Yeah, I guess you do now,' he murmured, the suggestive look making her sure he wasn't talking about swimming any more.

Apparently, their truce was over.

Before she could come up with a suitably non-confrontational response—and stop the heat from sinking any deeper into her sex—he had jumped out of the quad.

He slung his rucksack over a shoulder, then stacked a couple of her suitcases under his other arm. 'Grab what you can, and I'll come back for the rest.'

She lifted the biggest suitcase she could manage, not wanting to seem like a shirker, but wondering again where his staff were. Not that she minded carting her own luggage, but she was starting to become concerned about the silence… And that intense feeling of intimacy that had been so electrifying—and so problematic—the last time they'd been alone together.

'Open up.' He barked the command into the frosty air as they headed across the terrace. A glass panel slid open in the house's façade.

The electric door slid closed behind them as they entered the indoor space. The double-height living area was stunning, the glass walls giving them an unencumbered view of the frozen landscape, while the flames from a granite fireplace in the far wall threw a warm glow over the luxurious furnishings.

Isabelle spotted a strikingly modern kitchen on the other side of the living area—with bespoke wooden cabinetry and state-of-the-art appliances—but then she stopped dead. In the other corner of the living room was a ten-foot freshly cut fir tree, decorated with red silk ribbons, gold baubles and white fairy lights.

Emotion wrapped around her ribs, like a suffocating blanket, threatening to yank her back into the past, as the memories she had suppressed for so long, and so diligently, slammed into her and the scent of pine resin got trapped in her lungs.

'What's wrong?' The husky question from behind her—which was far too perceptive—made her jolt.

She blinked furiously, the twinkle of lights blurring, as she struggled to cut off the melancholy thoughts.

'Hey, are you crying?' he asked.

'No, of course not,' she said, but the denial sounded weak and unconvincing.

Biting into her cheek, she shoved the memories back into the box marked 'ancient history'. 'It's just... The tree is a surprise. I didn't think you would be the sort of person to have one,' she managed, struggling to cover her reaction.

He stared at her, for the longest time, and she had the awful suspicion he could see through the lie. But then he glanced past her at the cause of her distress. 'I guess Megan, my housekeeper, had it put up,' he murmured. 'I can take it down if it bugs you.'

*Yes, please.*

She swallowed the pathetic reply.

*Pull yourself together, Isabelle. It's just a tree, and a beautiful one.*

There were Christmas trees all over Androvia at this time of year—even if she never had one in her private quarters. She was used to seeing them and immune to their charm. She was just stressed and jet-lagged and had not been prepared to see one here, that was all.

'No, don't take it down. I like it. It's very festive. And I wouldn't want to insult your staff,' she managed. 'After all their hard work.' She pushed the words past the blockage in her throat.

He was still watching her, with that searing intensity, which made her feel transparent. But then his eyebrow quirked. 'I wouldn't worry about that. They won't know.'

'But aren't they here?' Isabelle blurted out, the silence pressing down on her.

'Nope,' he said, but his gaze remained fixed on her face. 'I always give my employees paid vacation from December twentieth until after New Year.' He was looking at her now with that vague sense of judgment. 'So they can enjoy some quality time with their families, instead of having to wait on me.'

'Oh…' Her lungs deflated, while emotion swelled in her throat and the fireball of need sank into her abdomen.

'What's the deal, Belle?' he said, making no attempt to hide his mockery now. 'Not used to cooking for yourself?'

She wanted to be indignant, insulted even, that he considered her position had made her spoilt and entitled. But all she could do was muster a vague embarrassment—beneath the wave of anxiety now holding her lungs in a death grip.

After all, he was correct—she had never cooked more than the most basic meals for herself, and that had been several years ago in college. But far worse than the realisation he thought so little of her was the news that for the next ten days she was going to be entirely alone with him.

And she would have nothing to do or think about other than her inability to look after herself, and how much his attention still disturbed and excited her.

What if having to celebrate the festive season with him risked exposing the vulnerable little girl again, behind the façade of competence and composure?

Had her fake honeymoon—which was always likely to be a challenge—just morphed into a full-blown Christmas nightmare?

'Could you show me to my room?' she asked, trying to keep her tone firm and even.

'You don't want anything to eat?' he asked.

She stared back at him blankly. Was he going to demand she cook a meal now? To test her culinary skills?

'I'm really not hungry,' she said, which was true, because her stomach was currently tying itself into tight greasy knots at the thought of what the next ten days had in store for her.

He shrugged. Then pointed past her shoulder. 'Elevator is over there. Guest rooms are all on the top level. Take your pick.'

She grasped her suitcase handle and began to wheel the bag to the lift.

'I'll be out boarding tomorrow. So, help yourself to food,' he called out, forcing her to turn again. 'The chef will have left some meals in the freezer, which you can nuke in the microwave,' he added, with that note of judgment she was already starting to hate. 'Feel free to check out the house. Pretty much everything is voice activated because I hate reading instructions.'

She nodded. From the rigid look on his face, she suspected he was regretting having to spend his Christmas alone with her now, too. But given he was the one who had insisted on putting them both in this untenable position, she had no sympathy for him—whatsoever.

She stored up the spurt of anger, hoping it would help fortify her for the days ahead.

'Thank you,' she said politely, because good manners had always been the shield she used to hide wayward emotions. And inappropriate urges.

A cynical knowing smile edged his lips.

And too late, she remembered her handy shield was about as useful as a thimble of water in an inferno when it came to not getting burned by her counterfeit husband.

'Relax, Belle. We agreed, this is a marriage without conjugal rights…' His gaze drifted down her figure, making her panic—and the curl of heat—flare alarmingly. 'But if you change your mind again, let me know. I'm always looking for an entertaining way to let off steam.'

'I won't,' she said, with a confidence she didn't feel but was determined to fake.

But as she turned her back on him again, the desire to hide until New Year from that mocking smile—and the hunger that refused to die—made her race towards the lift in another unseemly retreat.

# CHAPTER TWELVE

*Two days later*

TRAVIS DUMPED THE heavy snowboard in the mud room. He tugged off his boots, and his outer wear, ignoring the throbbing pain in his leg.

Once he got down to his shorts and T-shirt to examine the swollen knee though, he swore under his breath.

No wonder it hurt like a bitch.

He'd pushed himself way too hard over the last two days. Boarding from dawn to dusk, then working out in the pool or the gym like a madman to take the edge off a lot more than just his excess energy.

He chugged two heavy-duty painkillers. Keeping out of his wife's way—since that crack when they'd arrived had made her blush like a nun—had seemed like a smart move. He didn't know what had possessed him to bring up their one night together again, even as a joke. Perhaps he wasn't over the rejection as much as he thought. Because each day, after he'd exercised himself into a coma so he could sleep peacefully, he'd still woken up hard and ready for her.

He walked—or rather limped—through the house, heading for the kitchen and the ice machine. The tree lights glittered on the granite flooring, reminding him of her weird reaction when she'd spotted the fir on that first night.

What had that been about? Because he'd seen devastation in her eyes.

His heartbeat slowed. Now he thought about it, her private apartments in the palace had not been decorated, despite Androvia being the Christmas capital of Europe. Did she have some phobia about the season?

He'd considered taking the tree down the next morning. But in the end had decided against the idea. It would be a major job getting the ten-footer out of the house. And he liked it there, because it reminded him of how far he'd come since those Christmases with him and his mom when they'd had to settle for the last scraggy tree on the lot on Christmas Eve.

He should have asked Isabelle what the issue was, but they'd been avoiding each other since that first night— with him boarding all day and only returning to the house at nightfall, by which time she had escaped to her rooms.

He didn't even know if she'd used any of the facilities. The only signs she was even still here were the meals that had been disappearing, and the empty containers that appeared washed and stacked neatly on the sideboard each evening.

But from the state of his knee, it looked as if he was going to be housebound until after Christmas now. His heartbeat kicked up a notch at the thought of bumping into his invisible house guest. He probably ought to have a conversation with her about their plans for tomorrow, because it was Christmas Eve already and it looked like they were going to be stuck together tomorrow.

*Great.*

What did royalty do on Christmas? He hoped she wasn't expecting him to do the catering.

He huffed out an annoyed breath. It had always been just him and his mom on Christmas Day until that final Christmas before she'd died, when he'd messed up. The guilt and grief still hit him on the day itself, so he wasn't in the mood to socialise.

Having to spend the day with Belle wasn't going to make him feel any less raw, especially as he knew his mom would have chewed him out for ever agreeing to get married for a business opportunity in the first place.

Not for the first time, he wondered what his mom would have made of Belle.

He pushed down the prickle of disappointment when he found the living room and kitchen empty. Having to deal with her would only be more awkward while dealing with his bum knee.

But as he limped across the living area in the dusky light, a splash from outside had him scanning the pool terrace.

His heart stopped as Isabelle rose from the pool, her blonde hair tied in a knot, wearing just a couple of swatches of lace. Soaking-wet see-through lace, which reminded him of the panties he'd had his hand inside three days ago.

She tugged on a thick dressing gown and grabbed a towel lying on one of the heated loungers. Starting to shiver, she slid her feet into a pair of oversized slippers and shuffled across the terrace as fast as she could.

'Open the door, please,' she requested of the house's integrated system with her typical politeness.

The glass panel slid across, and then back, as she shot into the indoor space. She hadn't spotted him standing by the tree, his hands braced on the back of one of the couches to take the weight off his leg.

He stood there like a dummy, or the worst kind of peeping Tom, and watched as she shook out her hair. The curls fell in disarray onto her shoulders. His stomach muscles tightened, the familiar heat plunging south, at the memory of releasing her hair from the tangle of pins. The feel of the silky tresses, the sound of her groan as he massaged her scalp and the phantom scent of flowers and her assailed his senses all over again. And the pain in his knee moved north.

She looked as glorious now as she had on their wedding night. Young and fresh and approachable, without the regal reserve she so often cloaked herself with.

As she began to dry her legs with the towel, her full breasts—the rigid nipples poking through her wet bra—played peek-a-boo with the open robe.

She shivered again, then let out a soft laugh. His heart skipped several beats. And the tension in his gut cinched tighter, because her expression was a captivating combination of excitement, exhilaration and mischief—like a kid let out early from school on the first snow day of the semester.

This wasn't the controlled, unapproachable monarch, this wasn't even the forthright woman who had skewered him with her logic on the journey here and made him feel like a hot-tempered jerk… This was the other Isabelle, who hid behind both of those. The bold, impulsive girl who loved to ski too fast, who had the throwing arm of a Major League baseball pitcher, who kissed with a passion that could blow his head off—and who had come apart in his arms three nights ago.

His need—and his fascination—made him forget not

just the pain in his knee, but all the reasons why he didn't want her here.

The gruff chuckle came out before he could stop it. Her head rose, the towel slipping out of her hand as surprise crossed her features. But right there with it was the thrill of desire.

Yeah, she felt it, too. The livewire chemistry they'd been trying to ignore by avoiding each other.

'Travis,' she whispered, her expression wary as she gathered the robe, cutting off his view of all that delicious skin. 'You're back early.'

The fierce need charged through his veins as he watched her eyes darken with arousal.

He'd messed up. That night. They both had. But there had to be a way back from that. Because they had a week left, and he couldn't think of a better way to get them through a vacation period that they both seemed to have hang-ups about than feeding this incessant hunger.

'Yeah,' he said, the husky word scraping his throat. 'Great swimwear,' he added, loving the way her pale skin pinkened all the way to her hairline. 'But don't wear it for anyone but me.'

Isabelle stared at the man less than five feet away as hot yearning rushed over her chilled skin. He'd been gone yesterday morning at dawn and returned after dark—and as she'd roamed the house alone during the last two days, she had convinced herself his absence was for the best.

But as the ache in her breasts and the glorious heat in her sex pulsed, her heart turned over in her chest. Because she was happy to see him. Excited even.

'I didn't wear it for you,' she said, but the hoarse tone

and the thrust of her swollen nipples against her damp bra called her a liar.

She had been bored and stressed without him here—overthinking every aspect of their interactions so far. And miserable at the thought of spending another Christmas alone.

Because something about being in his home, with that huge Christmas tree here, had made the bad memories all the more acute.

'Oh, yeah.' His gaze raked down her body, which suddenly felt naked despite the heavy robe.

*It's just sex.*

The words echoed again, from that night, when she'd been scared… But not of him, she could see that now. What she had always been scared of was herself. And how much he could make her feel.

But what was she so terrified of? That this could mean more to her than it should? But why should it? When he had such a casual approach to physical intimacy? If it could be just sex for him, why couldn't it be for her?

Maybe he was right, maybe this would be a good way to make their relationship less stressful, not more so. There was no shame in sleeping with her own husband. And enjoying it. Their union was legal, even if not strictly speaking authentic.

'I didn't bring a swimsuit with me,' she explained, even as the riot of sensations was incinerating her self-control.

'Tsk-tsk,' he chastised her. 'Not very queenly of you to take a dip in your panties.'

She released her arms from around her waist, allowing the robe to fall open again, aware of his gaze gliding over her exposed skin.

She gathered every ounce of courage she had to flirt back. 'I thought you said you liked my swimwear.'

His gaze sharpened, even as the heat flared between them like a physical force, triggering an endorphin rush that felt as powerful as it was terrifying.

'Maybe take off the robe, Belle,' he mused. 'So I can review it properly.'

Exhilaration combined with panic as she peeled off the robe. It slid down her body to drop onto the warm stone flooring.

Her nipples were so hard they hurt, her breasts swollen and heavy, and the throbbing in her sex catastrophic.

'Come here,' he said, the rough command freeing her from the last of her inhibitions.

Stepping out of the slippers, she walked across the room barefoot. But as she reached him, he took his hands off the sofa, and stumbled.

'Damn it.' He bent to grip his leg.

'Travis, what's wrong?'

But as she came round the sofa, she could see the bruised, swollen flesh around his knee. And gasped.

He braced his hand back on the sofa. 'I just need some ice. It's nothing.'

It didn't look like nothing. But she stopped herself from saying as much because she could see the closed expression. Was he embarrassed at having shown a weakness in front of her?

'Let me get it.' All thoughts of seduction fled as she raced to the kitchen in her wet underwear.

By the time she had figured out how to work the refrigerator's ice machine and filled a freezer bag then wrapped it in a cloth, he had settled himself on the sofa and placed his leg on a leather footrest.

She perched next to him and placed the ice bag gently on the sore knee.

He flinched. 'Thanks,' he said, taking the bag and holding it on his knee.

'How did you do this?' she asked, horrified she had been thinking about sexual gratification while he must have been in agony. 'Did you fall? You should have told me you had injured yourself. I would never have—'

'It's okay, Belle,' he cut into the panic babble. 'I'm not gonna die from a swollen cruciate ligament… It's an old injury. The painkillers will kick in soon.'

So the swelling was a legacy of the accident that had destroyed his snowboarding career. Sympathy for him and the injury that had robbed him of so much engulfed her. But before she could offer him her condolences, he brushed the swollen peak pressing against the lace of her bra with his thumb.

She jolted, the dart of pleasure from the light touch immense.

'The sexual frustration, on the other hand…' he murmured, the erotic pull in his voice delving deep into her sex. As he played with her, skimming his thumb under her breast, and making her breathing accelerate, a sensual smile spread across his face. 'Could definitely kill me.'

'I feel dreadful,' she said, confused now as well as embarrassed.

'What for?' he said. 'Distracting me?'

He shifted in his seat. And she noticed the impressive bulge in his shorts. He was wearing another pair of those stretchy boxers she remembered from their wedding night—which left absolutely nothing to the imagination.

'In fact, you're still doing a great job of distracting me.'

'I should put my robe back on,' she said, suddenly aware she was practically naked... And so was he. 'You're in no condition to pursue this now,' she said, attempting to be the sensible one.

But as she went to get off the couch, he snagged her wrist. 'Don't,' he murmured.

The smile had gone, the intensity in his expression bringing the riot of sensations back with a vengeance.

She shivered, but it had nothing to do with her wet underwear.

His thumb pressed the thundering pulse point on her wrist. Making her brutally aware of the one still throbbing in her sex.

'Fire higher,' he commanded. Warmth enveloped her as the banked flames in the firepit flared. Orange flickers reflected in the dark brown of his irises, turning them to a rich chocolate.

'I'm in the perfect condition to pursue this, Belle,' he said his voice hoarse with need now. 'I want to touch you.'

It didn't sound like a question. 'But what about your knee?' she asked. 'I don't want to take advantage of you.'

His eyebrows rose up his forehead, then he chuckled. 'I'd love you to take advantage of me,' he said, the fierce light in his eyes brooking no more arguments. 'But you need to know, stopping again might be a problem this time...'

'I... I understand,' she said. And for once she did.

This really didn't have to be a big deal. At all. She'd made too much of the sex part of the equation, because of her inexperience. More than anything she wanted to see this through now, if only to defuse this terrifying need.

'But just so you know,' he added. 'It's not my knee that hurts right now.'

'I'm glad,' she said.

His eyes flared, dazzling her, as his grin became more than a little feral. 'Me too,' he murmured.

Shifting, he slipped one fingertip under her bra strap, eased it off her shoulder. Then dealt with the other. 'You want to unhook it, Belle?' he asked. 'As much as I like the improvised swimwear, I'd prefer you out of it.'

She stood, her heart pressing into her throat. Clumsily, she released the hook and peeled off the wet lace. His gaze intensified and he let out an unsteady breath as the bra dropped to the floor.

'You're stunning,' he murmured.

Her confidence swelled, along with the heat in her abdomen.

She could do this. However inexperienced she was, she could make him ache, too. The thought was so empowering, her excitement soared.

He patted one muscular thigh. 'Sit on my lap.'

'But won't that hurt your leg?'

'Belle,' he said, his expression rueful. 'Believe me, you'll hurt me a lot more if you don't.'

She choked out a laugh. 'Okay, if you're sure.'

She stepped over him, careful not to jar his sore leg, and settled on top of him, aware of the thick ridge pressing against the molten spot in her panties.

He groaned as she found herself rubbing against it. 'Careful,' he said. 'Or this is going to be over too soon.'

'Oh… I'm sorry,' she said, trying to shift back. But he banded one strong arm around her hips, holding her in place.

'No, you don't,' he murmured, then pulled her closer, to capture one stiff peak between firm lips.

She gasped as he suckled her yearning flesh. The drawing sensation arrowed into her sex, and her back arched, instinctively offering him more. Offering him everything.

He lathed and sucked, playing with one peak and then the other, trapping the swollen flesh against the roof of his mouth, to increase the devastating suction. Until she was rocking against his hips, desperate for relief as the waves climbed higher. And the heat coiled tighter at her core.

His hands found her bottom, those sure fingers diving beneath her panties, until she was riding his lap. She clung to his shoulders, aware of the iron bar in his shorts, pressing against the perfect spot. Liquid heat exploded along her nerve-endings, making her cry out.

She threw her head back as the orgasm ripped through her, fast and furious and unstoppable.

The pleasure battered her until all that was left was the glittering sensation. And the mindless drop into afterglow.

She drifted down, her whole body quivering and humming.

'Damn but you're glorious when you come,' he groaned.

Her eyes opened, to find him watching her with a harsh possessive fury in his eyes that seared her soul.

He pressed his lips to hers in a sensual, provocative kiss.

'Good?' he asked, his large palm stroking her hip.

She nodded. 'Incredible… I've never…' She caught herself just in time, before she blurted out the awful truth. That no one had ever made her feel the way he did. But her heart lurched, thumping her ribs when he smiled lazily.

*Just endorphins, Issy. Just sex...*

'You've never what?' he asked.

'I never expected us to be so good together...' she lied, trying to sound as if he hadn't just blown her mind again—completely. And he wasn't the first man to ever make her want so much.

One dark eyebrow hiked up his forehead. 'I figured it was kind of obvious from our wedding night we had some serious chemistry...'

She shifted, suddenly uneasy at how much he saw. And how needy—and exposed—she felt.

She glanced down, aware of the thick erection—still rigid between her thighs.

'What do you want me to do...?' She paused, cleared her throat, the fierce longing—at the sight of him, so large and hard, for her—not helping her to appear nonchalant, and sophisticated... And not completely overwhelmed.

He let out a strained chuckle, and placed a kiss on her nose, the affectionate gesture not helping with the dryness in her throat, or the thunder of her pulse.

'I want to be inside you,' he murmured. 'But first I'm going to have to limp up to my bedroom and find the condoms.'

'You don't need them,' she blurted out. Then realised her mistake when his brow furrowed.

'How come?'

'I'm... I'm on the pill,' she offered, forced to come clean about the lie.

He tilted his head to one side, then lifted one hand to rub her reddened nipple. 'How long have you been on it? Are you sure we're protected?'

'I... Yes.' She jolted against that possessive caress, the

last of her fear washed away on the wave of longing. 'I was prescribed contraceptives when I was seventeen, because my cycle was so erratic and the cramps could be crippling.' The words came out in a rush, the stream of too much information a way to stave off the nerves, and to prevent more questions.

'My cycle began to impede my schedule of engagements, so the mini pill was considered an effective way to manage my menstruation better and prevent the prospect of having to cancel anything at the last minute… I'm sorry I lied. I…'

'Shh. It's okay, Belle.' He brushed his thumb across her lips, the fierce need in his eyes—which hadn't faded— making the strange feeling of connection press against her ribs. 'I get it,' he added. 'You weren't ready on our wedding night. All I need to know is that you are now.'

She swallowed past the lump of emotion. It was a practical question about consent, nothing more. 'I… Yes, I am.'

He kissed her again, even as his palm landed on her bottom, and edged under her panties. 'Then we need to be wearing less clothing.'

'Oh, yes, of course.' She stood to take off her panties, embarrassed at her gaucheness but trying hard to keep the latest spurt of panic at bay.

But when she turned back to him, he had lost the T-shirt and eased down his shorts… Her heart bounced into her throat and became wedged between her thighs simultaneously.

*Oh, my.*

She let her gaze drift over his physique, attempting to gather her wits and slow her racing pulse as she took in the strong bulge of muscle and sinew, the toned, tanned flesh, the small scars and imperfections—which only added to the savage masculine beauty of his body. The name tattooed across his pec still fascinated her, as well as the sprinkle of hair that surrounded his nipples, then tapered into a line through washboard abs, which were even more magnificent now, gilded in firelight.

'You want to sit back on my lap?' he prompted.

Her gaze lifted to his amused expression. Fire scorched her cheeks. Could he see, did he know, she had never done this before?

*Just get on with it, then, Issy.*

She forced a smile to her own lips.

'I'm just admiring the view first,' she managed. Then reached out to touch him.

He sucked in a breath, his stomach tensing. The long, thick erection thrust upwards, as if it had a life of its own. Had it got even bigger in the last few seconds?

'You may have to hurry up,' he muttered, his voice strained. 'Or I'm seriously gonna embarrass myself here.'

The pained announcement had her own embarrassment fading, to be replaced by the surge of power.

*This isn't hard, Issy, stop overthinking this and go with your instincts.*

Luckily, she had a lot of instincts where he was concerned.

She trailed her fingers through his abs—loving the tensile strength, the feel of his skin, soft and warm. She circled a small tattoo on his hip flexor, the badge of the world snowboarding logo somehow captivating her, then—biting into her lip—lifted her finger to touch the bulbous head of his erection.

It jerked towards her touch. She sucked in a breath as he groaned, and a bead of moisture appeared at the tip.

She circled the thick girth, captivated by the velvet softness of his skin, and the contrast with the steel beneath. Her breath clogged in her lungs as she rubbed her thumb across the head. His hips rose and she felt the answering pull in her sex.

What was it going to feel like, to have all that hardness, that length and girth, inside her? It had felt so good with just his finger, but suddenly the urge to feel all of him—as he took her for the first time—was fierce and intense.

She bit harder into her lip as her fingers surrounded him, then drew her fist up and down the thick length, aware of his breathing becoming heavier, and harsher, and more urgent.

But then he gripped her wrist. 'As much as I'm enjoying that, we need to get to the main event, Belle, before I explode.'

She nodded. And climbed over his lap again, the feeling of power and excitement strengthening her resolve. She sucked in a lungful of his scent—the delicious musk of cedarwood and salt. Going with her instincts, she leaned forward and placed her mouth on his.

He clasped the back of her head and took over, thrusting his tongue deep, even as he lifted her hips and positioned himself at her entrance. She flinched, the pressure at her core painful, but the slickness of her recent orgasm allowed him to slide deep in one thrust.

She groaned, impaled to the hilt.

He swore softly, breaking the kiss. 'You're so tight,' he said, the strain in his voice making her aware of how close to the edge he was too. 'Are you okay? I'm not hurting you?'

She pressed her face into his neck, her breaths coming out in ragged pants as she struggled to adjust to the pressure, to ease the pain, aware of him so thick inside her, the full, stretched feeling too much.

His fingers threaded into her hair, to pull her head back and force her to meet his gaze. 'Damn it, Belle, are you a virgin?'

She blinked, wanting to deny it, but he must have seen the truth before she could find the lie.

He let out a stream of curses and dropped his head back against the sofa.

'I… I'm sorry,' she managed, ashamed now, as well as sore. But when she tried to lift off him he clasped her hips to keep her in place.

'Don't… Don't move.'

'But I thought—' she began.

'You should have told me, Belle,' he interrupted her again, the flicker of deep emotion stunning her into silence. 'But it's done now, and there's no undoing it.'

Was he angry with her? It was impossible to tell, and hard to concentrate on anything but the overwhelming feeling of having him inside her. Her sex throbbed, and burned, but when he shifted slightly, fierce pleasure pierced the tenderness.

'Tell me what you need,' he said, his voice rough with urgency now.

'Honestly, I don't know,' she replied, hideously exposed.

He swore again, but then he touched his forehead to hers. 'You're crucifying me here, Belle,' he whispered, the tone as raw as she felt.

She wanted to say something, anything. But it was all *too* much.

He cupped her cheek. 'Can you move?' he asked. 'Without hurting yourself more?'

'It doesn't hurt so much now,' she managed.

'That's good,' he said, the strain in his voice helping to ease her anxiety about his reaction. 'Why don't you take the lead, then?'

'How…? How do you mean?'

His eyes darkened, his focus on her—and only her—making her lungs seize.

Slowly he lifted her hips. Then eased her back down. The renewed jolt of pleasure rippled all the way to her toes.

'Good?' he asked.

'Yes… Good.'

'Then let's do that again. You decide how fast, how far you want to go. Whatever feels good, okay?'

'But what about you?'

He groaned. 'Don't worry about me. I'm just trying to hang on long enough to give you an orgasm before I lose it completely.'

He looked dazed, drained, and even though the vicious need still pulsed inside her—desperate to be filled—the wave of accomplishment at seeing what she did to him was its own reward.

She eased off him again, then sank back to the hilt. He was still huge, still overwhelming inside her, but the ripples began to build and merge as her clumsy movements became more focussed, more sure.

He moved with her, surging up as she sank down. And gradually, the exquisite pain turned to brutal pleasure.

He reached down to where they joined, finding the heart of her. And the hard pulse of pleasure rose again, harder, faster, more furious, more desperate.

He worked the spot, even as he grew larger inside her—his grunts matching her sobs. The heady wave of sensation rose to slam into her at last. She tumbled over into the abyss, her cries of completion followed by his shout of climax.

She collapsed into his arms, spent now, and worn out.

He shifted against her as she listened to the strong steady beat against her ear—the afterglow like a drug.

Was it supposed to feel this intense? As if she had been changed for ever? How did anyone survive something this intimate without losing their sense of self?

'You good?' he asked, not for the first time. But his voice sounded distant, lacking the playfulness and then the fierce passion she had found so beguiling.

She lifted her head off his chest, shocked by the painful clutch of emotion making her ribs hurt. A chill swept through her at his shuttered expression.

He settled his hand on her back, but the touch felt impersonal somehow. 'You need to dismount,' he said. 'My leg's starting to ache.'

Brutal humiliation chased away the last of the golden glow.

She climbed off his lap, the tenderness in her sex nothing compared to the sore spot in her heart. She scooped up the robe, feeling awkward and unsure, and more naked than she ever had before.

How could she have been so naïve to believe that throwing herself at this man, having sex with him, would be a simple fix?

He had stood up and put his T-shirt and shorts back on by the time she had tugged on her panties under the robe. But as she went to pass him, to escape to her room, he grasped her wrist.

'Not so fast, Belle,' he said.

'I... I need to shower,' she replied, trying to tug her arm loose.

'Don't you think we ought to have a conversation first?' he asked, but as before it wasn't really a question.

'About what?' she said, but she already knew from the frown on his face.

'You know what about,' he said. 'Why didn't you tell me you were a virgin until I was inside you?'

She heard it then, the suspicion in his voice, alongside the frustration. She forced herself to push the guilt to one side—and that old familiar feeling of inadequacy that she had spent so much of her childhood conquering.

'I didn't think you would care,' she replied, even though it wasn't entirely the truth. She hadn't thought about his re-action because she'd believed she could hide her inexperi-ence, that he wouldn't know, that he wouldn't find out. But why had she been so scared of him discovering the truth? What exactly was she so ashamed of?

'Seriously?' he said, the brittle cynicism cutting. 'You don't think I deserved to know, before I'd done something I couldn't undo?'

She heard it then, the note of accusation, as if she'd tricked him somehow.

Her own temper sparked, burning away some of the guilt and anxiety. Surely her sexual history was her own to divulge, as she chose. And what exactly was he accus-ing her of?

'If you didn't enjoy it,' she announced through gritted teeth, 'I apologise.'

Maybe she'd done something wrong. It wouldn't be the first time—given the disastrous way their wedding night had ended. But she refused to stand here and let him make her feel less than.

'You know damn well I enjoyed it,' he all but snarled. 'You practically blew my head off. That's not the point.'

The pulse of heat at his back-handed praise only upset and confused her more.

'Well, what *is* the point, then, Travis?' She threw the words back at him to cover the emptiness inside her, and the hum of arousal that made her feel like a fool.

'The point is, we were just supposed to be blowing off steam here, but now this… This…' He jerked his thumb back and forth between them, his gaze dark with a turmoil of emotions. 'This *thing* between us is a much bigger deal. And you know it.'

She stared at him.

'Why is it?' she asked, hopelessly confused now as well as upset. Why was this a big deal for him?

'Because I don't seduce virgins, okay? Because that would make me an even bigger bastard than the son of a—' The words cut off abruptly, his tanned cheeks darkening with the flush of temper—and emotion.

He swore under his breath. Then raked unsteady fingers through his hair. 'Forget it.'

Her own anger faded, the shocked, unhappy expression on his face making him seem suddenly vulnerable.

He let go of her wrist and walked away from her, the slight limp making her empathy for him rise up to choke her as she recalled the way he had spoken with such disgust about the father he insisted he had no feelings for.

The man who had taken advantage of his mother by seducing her as a seventeen-year-old virgin.

He stood, alone, looking out at the dark snowy night,

his back ramrod-straight, his body rigid with tension. As he fought demons he had pretended not to care about a couple of days ago.

The urge to go to him, to help him conquer those demons, made her heart thunder against her ribs. But she stopped herself from giving in to that urge, however powerful.

The sex had already meant more than it should have—the emotional fall-out still churning inside her, too. And while a part of her wanted desperately to take that haunted, ashamed expression off his face, she knew she couldn't afford to make herself a part of his struggle. Especially as he had made it clear he didn't want her to.

So she simply said, 'I'm not seventeen, Travis. I'm twenty-two. And I understand this can never be more than just sex.'

He didn't respond, didn't turn around, his only reaction the way his back muscles tensed.

She turned and walked to the lift, without saying any more.

But as she washed the scent of him off her body in the guest room's power shower, the raw feeling remained. Her body felt sore, tender, and well used—but also more alive than it had ever felt before.

Worse somehow, though, was the painful regret—that she had hurt him somehow with her silence, without intending to—and that fierce yearning, to know him, to understand him and to nurture the strange connection between them, which she now knew had always been more than just physical for her.

It was a realisation that scared her to her core.

# CHAPTER THIRTEEN

TRAVIS FLIPPED THE grilled cheese sandwich in the pan, then stiffened as he heard a throat clear nervously behind him.

He turned to find the woman he'd been thinking about all night standing in the living area, looking guarded—and hot—in a pair of tailored pants and a simple sweater. She'd tied her hair in a ponytail, her fresh skin devoid of make-up… Which only made her look more artless. And innocent.

*Probably because she was, you chump.*

The fierce possessiveness that had freaked him out the night before hit him all over again.

'Good morning,' she said, with her perfect manners, which he now knew were a cover for an emotional intelligence he lacked.

He cleared his own throat. 'Hi,' he murmured. 'And merry Christmas.'

'Yes, merry Christmas,' she replied with about as much enthusiasm as he felt, which wasn't much.

He swung back to the stove and pulled the grilled cheese off the heat. He was a master of no-stress mornings after. Because he'd had a lot of practice at striking the perfect balance between 'I've had fun' and 'I'm out of here now'.

But he'd screwed up so badly last night, this threatened

to be the most awkward morning after in the history of the world ever.

He'd made an ass out of himself. He'd browbeaten Belle, when the person he'd really been mad with was himself. For not reading all the signs that had been staring him in the face since he'd met her.

The tentative, curious way she'd kissed him that first time in her office... The eager passion of their stunt kiss in Sariyelva—which hadn't felt like a stunt the minute he'd put his mouth on hers. The artless passion that had overwhelmed her on their wedding night, then the way she'd panicked and run out. Her vibrant, vivid but totally unstudied responses to him yesterday—which had blindsided them both.

He should have figured out he was the first guy to touch her—but he'd enjoyed her responses so damn much he'd chosen to ignore the signs to satisfy his own lust. So whose fault was it really that taking her virginity had turned this relationship into a much bigger deal than it was supposed to be, and turned him into as big a bastard as his old man?

'How is your knee?' she asked, the caution in her voice making him hate himself that much more.

'Good. How are you doing?' he asked. 'Not too sore?'

'Oh... No... It's... I'm fine,' she said, her cheeks lighting up like the Christmas tree behind her as the awkward quotient hit a hundred. 'You were very careful.'

'Not as careful as I should have been,' he murmured. 'And I behaved like a jackass afterwards,' he continued, trying to get the knots in his gut to untangle.

He could see he'd surprised her, even as she tried to cover her shock.

'Which is why I've got a peace offering for you this

morning,' he continued, sliding the grilled cheese sandwiches onto the plates he'd laid out on the breakfast bar.
'Take a load off and dig in.'

He took one of the stools on his side of the kitchen is-
land and pushed her plate and cutlery across to her side.

She hesitated, clearly unsure of his mood. He knew how
she felt. He wasn't super sure of his mood either. He'd never
felt this awkward or exposed before. But then he'd never
been a woman's first lover either.

'It's okay, Belle. I promise I won't bite you,' he said as
he grabbed his fork and started chunking up his sandwich.
'Not unless you ask me to,' he added, trying to lighten the
mood.

She blushed—because of course she did—but relief
crossed her features.

And he wanted to kick himself some more, for trying to
make her feel bad when he was the one who hadn't been
able to get his reaction to her virginity into perspective.

He wasn't even sure what had made him feel so raw.
Clearly, he had more hang-ups about his old man than he'd
ever realised. Plus, Christmas Day had always made him
feel kind of crap about himself after the way he'd treated his
mom that last Christmas. But even so, his knee-jerk freak-
out—and the weird surge of emotion that he was pretty sure
had helped trigger it—didn't make a whole lot of sense.

'I...' She paused again. 'Thank you,' she said graciously.
Then she climbed onto the stool opposite him. Relief
gushed through him. Maybe this didn't have to be that big
a deal after all. If he could just get last night into perspective again. She'd said it was just sex. And that was what
they both wanted. Wasn't it?

'I appreciate it,' she added, then lifted her knife and

fork and sliced off a corner of the sandwich. She tucked the bite-sized piece into her mouth—and licked the sheen of melted butter off her bottom lip. The inevitable bolt of lust shot straight into his groin.

He set about demolishing his own sandwich while ignoring it.

He finished way ahead of her and poured himself a cup of black coffee. 'You want some?' he asked, lifting the pot.

She nodded. He poured her a cup then pushed the cream and sugar her way and watched her add a generous helping of both to the coffee. She took a hefty sip, before tucking back into her sandwich. Making him wonder if her throat was as dry as his.

*Probably.*

'Thank you,' she said for about the tenth time between bites. 'This is absolutely delicious. What do you call it?'

His lips quirked, the question as cute as it was surprising. 'You're pretty sheltered, aren't you?' he said. Then felt like a jerk when she stiffened.

'Yes, I suppose I am,' she said with her typical honesty.

'Hey...' He reached across to place his hand over the fingers she had clenched tight on her fork. 'I didn't mean that as a criticism. Or an insult. Just an observation. Okay?'

She nodded, and her fingers relaxed. Resisting the urge to stroke the soft skin, he shoved his hand into the pocket of his sweatpants.

'It's grilled cheese on rye,' he said while she polished off the last of the sandwich. 'My mom taught me how to cook them when I was around seven. It was one of our favourites. I'd make them for both of us on Christmas morning and we'd eat them in our PJs. It was our favourite Christmas tradition—right up there with grabbing the last tree on the lot next to our trailer park and decorating it on Christmas Eve.' He paused, realising he was the one babbling now. 'So it felt appropriate today, that's all...' He trailed off, feeling kind of dumb. Why was he rambling on about his mom and their Christmas traditions? Especially as he hadn't even been there to cook the grilled cheese sandwiches she loved for her on her last Christmas because he'd been too busy being a selfish bastard to read the signs then, too.

'That sounds like so much fun,' Belle murmured, the understanding in her eyes something he knew he didn't deserve. 'You must miss her terribly, especially at Christmas, then.'

'Yeah.' He shrugged, uncomfortable with her sympathy. After all, she'd lost both her parents long before he'd lost his mom.

'Did you have a lot of Christmas traditions?' she asked, the warmth in her gaze turning her green eyes to a rich emerald.

'I guess. Doesn't everyone?' he said.

'Yes, I... I suppose they do,' she said, but the curiosity in her eyes died as her gaze slipped away from his—to land on the tree across the room.

Reaching across the bar, he covered her hand again.

Her head turned back to his.

'What's the issue with the tree?' he asked, aware of the unhappiness swirling in the emerald green even as she tried to mask it.

She drew her hand out from under his. 'Nothing.'

He propped his elbows on the bar and studied her face.

'You do know you're a crummy liar, right?' he countered, and her face went an interesting shade of pink. 'Is

Christmas when you lost your folks?' he probed, wanting to know what had put that wistful look in her eyes.

Which was a novel experience for him—normally he wouldn't be interested in figuring out what made a woman tick.

But Belle had always been different. She fascinated him on so many different levels. Not just the livewire chemistry they shared, or that captivating innocence—his OTT reaction to which he was still trying to figure out—but also all her contrasts: the shyness behind the competence, the innocence beneath the reserve, and all those tantalising glimpses of the reckless girl, the vulnerable woman behind the mask of the confident queen.

'No, they died in a helicopter crash right before my ninth birthday in July,' she said.

'That must have been really tough,' he said, his chest tightening at her carefully guarded expression. He knew what that felt like, trying to hold it together, so no one could see you bleed.

'Yes, the country went into deep mourning. It was a dreadful day for Androvia,' she said, her voice still carefully devoid of emotion. 'They were both such exemplary monarchs—always so focussed on their duty to the throne. I'm not sure the country and its citizens have ever really recovered from the loss.'

He frowned. 'I meant, it must have been tough for you. You were just a little kid. And you'd lost both your parents.'

Her brows rose slightly, almost as if she were surprised at the question. 'Yes, but...' She paused. 'Of course, I missed them terribly,' she said, but her voice sounded hollow, almost as if she was trying to persuade herself. 'But ultimately, I was glad they died together, as they loved each other very much.'

*Huh?*

It was Travis's turn to frown. Wasn't that sentiment way too mature for a kid of eight? But he could see from the brave acceptance in her gaze she had come to terms with her loss a long time ago. Then again…

'So, what's the deal with the tree, then?' he asked. Even curiouser now. Surely it had to be something to do with her childhood, because he'd sensed her lack of sentimentality about the season right from the start.

'It's nothing,' she said. But then she shrugged and stared down at her plate, to toy with the last bite of her grilled cheese. 'It's silly, really.'

And then he knew it wasn't nothing—because she wasn't meeting his eye, and he knew that was the tactic she used when she couldn't hide her emotions behind the shield of manners.

'Is it nothing, or is it silly? Because it can't be both,' he asked gently, curious now not just about the woman, but also the little girl. Had she covered her grief then too, behind a shield of polite conformity? And duty.

The thought made him sad for her. And angry.

Shouldn't every kid be allowed to act out, especially at a time like that? She would have been thrust into the public eye even more after her parents' death. The pressure to be perfect would have been a massive burden. Had they ever even given her a chance to grieve? And how could she not have buckled under the strain?

Her gaze met his at last. 'Honestly, it's very silly and also quite self-indulgent. I'm embarrassed to talk about it.'

'Try me,' he said, beginning to wonder if she had always

thought her feelings, her needs, were less important than her duty to the Androvian throne.

Because it was certainly starting to look that way.

Why else would she have suggested marrying a total stranger? When she'd never even had a proper relationship before now. Never even dated.

Did she have any idea how damn vulnerable she was? Especially to a guy like him.

A man who had spent his whole life taking what he wanted, when he wanted it, without a thought to how it might impact anyone else. Not even his own mom. While she'd subjugated her own desires to assume the burden of a whole country's expectations when she was only eight. He'd always been proud of how single-minded he was, how he'd always kept his eyes on the prize, his take-no-prisoners approach to everything from his business to his love life. But his drive and ambition were starting to look kind of selfish now, compared with her loyalty and dedication to her subjects and her country and her parents' legacy.

She gave an impatient huff. 'Okay, but you must promise you won't laugh, or think less of me,' she said.

'Yeah, that's not gonna happen,' he said. But when she sent him a sceptical look, he crossed his little finger over his heart and kissed the tip. 'Pinkie swear.'

Her gaze strayed back to the decorated tree across the room. 'Seeing Christmas trees, all lit up like that...' She gave a wistful sigh. 'They're so festive and bright, but they make me feel so lonely. Which is ridiculous, of course.'

Why was it ridiculous? 'Do you know the reason why they make you feel that way?'

'Yes,' she said without hesitation. 'The reason is even sillier actually. And also very selfish... I used to get terribly upset when I was a child that my parents couldn't be with me on Christmas Day.'

'That's not dumb at all,' he said, vehemently defending feelings she seemed unable to defend herself. 'Of course you missed them. I still miss my mom on Christmas Day and she's been gone for over a decade.'

She turned to him, her cheeks reddening. 'You misunderstand. This was before they died. Christmas was very important to them as a couple. They loved each other very much and they got so little time to spend together, because they had such busy schedules. My father explained to me the three days over Christmas were very precious—and the only time they could spend together just the two of them—which was why they left me at the palace with the staff on Christmas Eve. But I always cried anyway. He would get annoyed with me, making such an unnecessary scene. And now that's one of the few memories I have left of him—which is awful really.'

'You're not serious?' he murmured, his voice tight with shock—and anger for that kid who had been gaslighted by her own dad. 'Who the hell leaves their only kid home alone at Christmas, so he can go off on a three-day booty call with his wife?'

Her eyebrows launched up her forehead, her cheeks darkening, but at least he'd shocked the guilt right out of her eyes.

'You don't understand,' she said, the misplaced loyalty making him hate her father even more. 'That's not how it was at all.'

'The hell it isn't,' he said. Because he understood just fine. Not only had her old man left that dumb instruction in his will that had forced her to marry, but he hadn't even stuck around for Christmas when she was a kid, and he'd taken her mom off with him. Leaving his daughter with nobody but people who were paid to be there. 'Your father sounds like an even bigger jerk than mine, and that's saying something.'

'But you're wrong,' she said, although she didn't sound quite as sure any more. 'Obviously, he loved me very much,' she added. 'And after their death Mel and her mother came into my life and that helped immeasurably. We became such good friends, even though we are quite different. Of course, they couldn't spend Christmas with me either,' she added, in that matter-of-fact tone that didn't dim the sadness in her eyes. 'Because it was the only time Mel's mother could take her to visit their family in London. Maybe that is also why Christmas still makes me feel lonely, which is doubly selfish of me.'

'That's garbage, Belle,' he said, getting more annoyed by the second. 'Maybe Mel and her mom couldn't stay with you. But your father could have, and so could your mom. What you're describing isn't love, it's neglect. If you love someone, you spend time with them—you make memories that matter with them. My mom worked three jobs, but she never missed a single competition I was in. And we always spent Christmas Day together. Just the two of us.'

The anger twisted in his gut, becoming sour and bitter as it turned inward. And he recalled his mom's email to him that last Christmas—every word of which he still remembered with crystal clarity.

Travis, honey, will you be able to make it back for the twenty-fifth? I'd love to see you if you can. But don't sweat it if you can't. I've put the enormous spruce you sent me

and all the presents in pride of place in my new lounge.
I intend to decorate the tree tomorrow, now I'm finally
over the chemo. Knock 'em dead on the half-pipe, that
title is already yours.

Love Mom x

The courage and selflessness in that email still sick-
ened him.

Who was he to judge her old man, or his own, when he
was just as much of a selfish jerk?

'Except her last Christmas,' he blurted out, not sure why
he was confessing to her.

But when he saw the misguided sympathy cloud her eyes
again, he knew why.

Isabelle's selflessness—her willingness to blame herself for something that had never been her fault—put his
own selfishness into context. Plus, it was way past time he
confronted the crappy way he'd behaved back then—to the
only woman who had ever made the mistake of loving him.

'She must have known the cancer was terminal,' he said,
the guilt twisting in his gut, the hideous fear and panic after
that initial diagnosis still there after all these years. 'But
I was way too focussed on winning some dumb competition to notice what was right in front of my eyes. I didn't
ask about her prognosis, because I was scared to hear the
answer. So, I stayed in France over that whole Christmas,
convincing myself I needed the extra time in training to
work on my jumps. But the real reason was that I didn't
want to go home and watch her struggle. I didn't want to
have to confront the truth. It was cowardly and mean. And
I still regret it. Which is why I'm not much fun to be around
at Christmas either.'

Instead of seeing what he was trying to tell her—about what selfishness really looked like—Isabelle's eyes darkened even more, with a compassion he had no right to.

She reached out and clasped the hand he had resting on the bar. 'But, Travis, you were just a boy. And she was so important to you. Of course you were terrified,' she said, the empathy in her voice rich with emotion.

He tugged his hand free to cup her cheek, feeling her tiny shiver of awareness. And wished, if only for a moment, he could be a better man. A man worthy of a woman like her.

Not the queen, but the woman beneath. Her loyalty to the people she loved could never be shaken, even when they didn't deserve it. She was much stronger than he had ever been.

'Don't feel sorry for me, Belle,' he said. 'I don't deserve it.'

She opened her mouth to protest, but he slid his thumb across her bottom lip to stop her. And felt her delicious shudder.

'The point is, if your folks had *really* loved you, if they had deserved you, they wouldn't have abandoned you like that,' he said. 'They would have stuck around to be with you. Especially at Christmas.'

Just as he should have stuck around for his mom.

'That they didn't is on them. Not you,' he finished.

The glitter of tears in her eyes crucified him a little more, especially when she eased out an unsteady breath and nodded. 'I guess… Yes, perhaps they really shouldn't have been quite so willing to leave me like that,' she said. The sadness was still there, but somehow the hopelessness was gone.

He was glad.

'Ya think?' he murmured, and she smiled, the bright sweet smile that lit up her whole face.

'Come on,' he said, walking round the breakfast bar to grab her arm, suddenly determined to make this Christmas the best she'd ever had—which wasn't going to be much of a challenge, by the sound of it. After all, it was the least he could do after the crummy way he'd treated her, too.

'I can't go nuts today thanks to my bum knee,' he said. And as much as he would love to, they couldn't lose themselves in sex either, because she was probably still a little sore. Although he saw no reason not to make the most of this chemistry now they had come to an agreement about what this meant and what it didn't. 'But how about I teach you how to snowboard so we can both get through today without any more drama? I've got some spare kit you can use.'

Her eyes gleamed, the sparkle of excitement as captivating as it was refreshing. 'Actually, I think I would like that very much,' she said.

His own excitement soared. But as he dragged her into the mud room, to get them both tooled up, he could almost feel his mom looking down on them both and hear her voice—her tone loving, and supportive, but also well aware of all his flaws.

*About damn time you stopped moping around, Travis. I swear, what are Christmases for but to have fun? You've wasted far too many of them since I've been gone.*

As they messed about in the snow for the rest of the day, the guilt that had crippled him at Christmas for so long let go its hold on him. Because they ended up creating new memories, full of laughter, while they wrestled together in the snow, and he taught her the basics of boarding while trying to prevent them both from falling on their asses.

But that night, while they stripped off in front of the fire—and he watched her give herself over to the explosive passion they shared—the emotion he still didn't understand, that surge of protectiveness and possessiveness, blindsided him all over again.

And scared the heck out of him. Again.

# CHAPTER FOURTEEN

*One week later*

'HOLD ON, BELLE, don't go over yet. I want you with me this time...'

Travis's harsh demand brushed against Isabelle's ear as his strong arms held her upright, and his driving thrusts impaled her.

'I can't... It's too much.' She panted, clinging to his shoulders, and tried to prevent the wall of pleasure from barrelling towards her at breakneck speed.

'Yes, you can,' he demanded, still thrusting heavily inside her, working all the places he had discovered over the past week that would trigger her release.

Her back thudded softly against the stone of the power shower. She threw her head back, stared up through the room's glass ceiling, and the sprinkle of snow in the night sky, and tried to focus on holding back, holding on. But the coil drew tighter as the heavy thrusts became faster and more frantic.

Her skin sparkled and glowed, still alive from the steam room, and the cold plunge before they had ended up in the shower... And things had heated up even more.

\* \* \*

But she couldn't focus on anything but the power of him, stretching her, pushing her, remaking her, caressing that spot inside her that ached for him, always.

Her sex tightened and pulsed, clamping down on his as the unstoppable pleasure crested, bright, beautiful and never-ending, bursting through her body.

She sobbed as the brutal release overwhelmed her.

'Yes!' he shouted out, climaxing too, as they flew over together.

The storm of sensation sent her tumbling into the abyss she had become addicted to in the last week and the only thing tethering her to the earth was him.

'Water off.' He barked out the command.

She flinched, as she released the still firm erection with difficulty.

'You good?' he murmured, as he so often did, while holding her.

Her heart swelled in her chest as she nodded, but she kept her eyes closed, the emotions still swirling inside her—incandescent joy followed by crippling fear.

A reaction she knew she needed to contain—if she didn't want to lose even more of herself.

*Just sex, just endorphins, no biggie.*

She tightened her arms around his neck, too wobbly and needy to stand as he carried her out of the shower. She buried her head against his shoulder, waiting to regain her equilibrium, and the sense of self she always seemed to lose in his arms. But as she breathed in the delicious scent of cedar and soap and he held her so securely, so tenderly, her heart grew so big it began to push against her throat.

He put her on her feet beside the vanity to grab them both a towel.

She stumbled and he grasped her arm. 'You okay?'

'Yes, of course.' She braced her knees and wrapped a warm towel around her aching body, still too tender. And exposed.

He hooked a towel around his waist as she crossed to the door, needing the safety and security of her own bedroom—the bedroom she'd abandoned a week ago. But before she could make her escape, he grasped her arm.

'Hey, where are you off to so fast?' he asked, calmly.

*Too* calmly, while her heartbeat continued to rabbit in her chest. And scour her throat.

How could he be so collected, so casual, she wondered, when she was always in bits after they made love? And how could their physical connection have become even more intense—for her at least—when she had been trying to wean herself off the endorphin fix for days?

'I should sleep in my own room tonight,' she said, taking the coward's way out, even as the pain in her chest refused to subside. 'We have a long day ahead of us tomorrow and I need to pack.' The thought of which suddenly seemed overwhelming, too.

'Don't go,' he said, tugging her around, his rough palm warm on her cheek. 'It's our last night here before we have to return to the circus,' he murmured, with the sting of bitterness that had begun to disturb her, too.

They'd spoken a few times over the past week about the duties he would need to perform as her consort once they returned to Androvia. But there had been so little time for the practical—in between their hastily prepared meals, the days spent out on the slopes messing about in the snow like carefree children, and the increasingly intense bouts of lovemaking.

She understood his reluctance, of course, because she had been guilty of avoiding those conversations, too—to indulge in all the ways he could make her feel so good.

The sex had been a revelation for her. She had never imagined she would find it so energising and exhausting and yet also so utterly addictive. Every time he looked at her now with that hooded gaze, the desire in his eyes unmistakable, she could feel her body softening as it prepared itself for him…

But as the riot of sensations rippled over her skin again, her body no longer felt like her own.

Why couldn't she resist him, or the things he could do to her? Or control the increasingly confusing emotions making her ache for so much more than just sex?

Ever since their conversation on Christmas Day, when he had given her an insight into his close relationship with his mother—and made her realise she had never been to blame for her distant relationship with her own parents—the insatiable need to know more about him had grown and grown. Until she had become desperate to know everything.

But when she'd probed, however gently, in the days since, he'd studiously resisted any more personal conversations—making her feel alone even as she lay in his arms, listening to his heart thud against her ear, steeped in afterglow.

Somehow, he had rediscovered that needy little girl, and reawakened the foolish yearning for the closeness her parents had always denied her. But she couldn't risk threatening their friendship—and the working relationship they would need to establish going forward—so she needed to start resurrecting her boundaries.

'I thought I'd sling a couple of steaks on the grill and we could watch a movie in the cinema suite tonight. Your pick. And celebrate the New Year together...'

His smile was warm and so inviting, but the distance remained in his eyes, which she had noticed more and more over the last few days, every time they made love...

The distance she should be establishing, too.

Why then did she still feel the vicious dart of disappointment and regret at the thought of saying no to him now? And the dull ache of sadness—because she couldn't help reading far too much into the casual suggestion.

*Is this what love feels like?*

The question that had been lurking in her subconscious for days popped out without warning.

Surely, she could not be so foolish? So naïve? This was just the endorphin overload talking too, it had to be.

'I'm really not hungry,' she managed, backing away from him. 'And I think it's probably best we sleep apart from now on. Plus, I need to contact Mel and thank her,' she began to babble, the familiar anxiety rising up to tangle with her panic as she headed to the door. 'I had to ask her to host tonight's New Year's Eve ball with Rene, who is not one of her favourite people.'

Rene and she always hosted the Saltzaland New Year's Eve event together, in a symbolic celebration of the close union between their two countries. Mel never attended because she usually took the opportunity to spend some vacation time away from Androvia over Christmas and New Year —either in London with her mother who was now retired, or elsewhere. It was just one of the many favours

Isabelle had been forced to ask of the people close to her, the palace staff and her privy council, to accommodate this honeymoon.

The honeymoon that now felt far too real.

Guilt pushed at her throat—because she hadn't thought of Mel, or Rene or even of Androvia since Christmas Day, jettisoning all her responsibilities far too easily too.

A call to Mel—to get a debriefing on the event which would be finished now given the time difference and catch up with her closest friend—would surely help to ground her again. Get this past week back in perspective. And prepare her for a return to her real life.

She couldn't be in love with Travis Lord. She was just tired and struggling to cope with a host of new emotions in the past week that were way outside her realm of experience. Travis had mentioned how sheltered she was, and in many ways he was right. Her life had always been studiously planned and managed. She simply wasn't accustomed to having to deal with anyone this exclusively on a daily basis, for this length of time, with no schedule or other distractions to focus on—while also discovering she had an insatiable sex drive.

She had to start getting these volatile yearnings under control—and build a working relationship with her fake husband for *after* their honeymoon that wouldn't distract her from her priorities.

She'd binged on the strong sexual connection they shared, they both had, but how could she continue to be a slave to her newly discovered libido without losing sight of what their marriage was supposed to achieve? Her role as Queen had always been exceptionally demanding, and now she was legally able to take full control of her inheritance, it would only become more so.

But as she tried to make a speedy exit, Travis strode across the room behind her and slapped his palm on the door, slamming it shut.

'Wait up, Belle,' he murmured, his breath hot against her nape, the easy manner gone.

She turned in his arms, to find him leaning over her, his hand still braced on the door above her head, the dark frown on his face wary and intense.

She breathed in a lungful of his scent and turned away from the sight of his bare chest glistening with moisture from their shower—and the tattoo of his mother's name, which she had discovered he had had etched on his skin a few days after her death.

*He's a man who feels so much, but not for you.*

She swallowed down the pathetic thought—which reminded her of the child who had once begged her parents to stay, and watched them leave regardless.

Surely this reaction was exactly why she needed to get a grip.

'What did you mean by us sleeping apart from now on?' he asked, his tone strained. He grasped her chin and raised her face to his. 'Explain.'

She tugged her chin free, hideously aware of her body clenching and releasing at his nearness, even though he had given her several orgasms not five minutes ago. And the tremble of vulnerability, the wayward emotions she couldn't control.

'I think it is probably best we don't continue our sexual relationship when we return to Androvia…' She forced the words out past the aching pain in her throat and the deep feeling of loss in her chest. 'It will only complicate the working relationship we need to establish.'

His eyes flashed with something searing. But before she could gauge his reaction, he had dropped his arm and stepped back, his gaze becoming flat and emotionless.

'Yeah… I guess you're right.' His gaze roamed over her body, which felt naked now even under the thick towel. 'Too much sex is kind of distracting.'

Her heart shattered, the brittle tone, the assessing gaze as insulting as they were hurtful. And suddenly she was that little girl again… Rejected and alone.

She gave a stiff nod, blinking furiously—as she struggled to shore up the turmoil of emotions.

This was what she had wanted from him. To stop the yearning, to stop believing in the vain hope that more could be possible between them. He had simply told her what she already knew. Why on earth was she so devastated?

'I'm glad you understand,' she managed at last, before she shot out of the door.

But as she returned to her own room, and lay shivering, curled up under the covers, she couldn't seem to reconcile her duty to her throne with the empty space that had always been inside her, and had only ever been filled in his arms, but was now emptier than ever.

# CHAPTER FIFTEEN

'WHAT DO YOU mean you haven't heard from her, either?' Isabelle demanded as the anxiety that had been clawing at her throat for over twenty-four hours started to restrict her breathing.

The last day had been nothing short of horrendous. Returning to Androvia had been hard enough, the responsibility of monarchy weighing her down as soon as she stepped off Lord Culture's private jet on the White Palace airstrip, to be greeted by her staff and several members of the Ruling Council, all with new problems to solve, or duties to fulfil.

But it had been so much harder to leave Colorado—and the woman she had become in Travis's home—behind.

The days there had merged into one long escape from reality, which made her life now in Androvia seem like so much more of a burden than before. But far worse, she had plunged down the rabbit hole of believing she and Travis might have been able to build something more out of their relationship. Because she couldn't look at him now without the yearning coming back, not just the physical desire to be held, to enjoy the pleasure he could give her, but more than that.

How could she have allowed herself to become so reliant on his companionship, too?

They had generally avoided any thorny topics about their pasts—or their emotions—after Christmas Day, but even so, simply talking to him about the resort project, his business, the intricacies of her role in Androvia, which he had begun to show an interest in as the days wore on, had allowed her to share at least some of the burden for the first time in her life.

And she hadn't even realised how much that had meant to her until she had thrown it away in her panic, on their last night in Colorado.

But as she glared at Arne now, she had to believe she had made the right decision to end their intimate relationship. She couldn't rely on Travis, couldn't lean on him, couldn't risk confusing the endorphin rush of sex with the development of a real relationship. Because that would mean a commitment from him that he had made it clear he was not willing to give—from the way he had so easily accepted the end of their intimate relationship.

In the days since, he hadn't made any attempt to change her mind. As they'd left the house and travelled back to Europe on his jet, their conversations had been stilted and far too polite—which was ironic given how much his lack of boundaries had once unnerved her.

She had missed the casual touches—and his irreverent relaxed way of speaking to her most of all. Even more than the physical intimacy. But she had forced herself not to reach out to him simply because she felt lonely again.

But she had been unable to sleep again last night, knowing he was in the room on the other side of the bathroom. It had been a titanic effort not to knock on his door and beg him to make love to her again. Just one more time.

She needed her friend Mel. She had to offload about

all this. Because bottling it all up was only exhausting her more. But she hadn't been able to get in touch with her PA since she had left on her not-so-fake honeymoon with Travis. Mel always took a Christmas and New Year break—if not to see her mother, then to some sunny clime where she could get away from the winter—and Isabelle had always respected her privacy. But it was beyond odd that if Mel had chosen to take leave after the ball, she hadn't told anyone where she was going. Not even Arne, who was in charge of the palace personnel and their schedules.

'Her phone has not been answered since the New Year Ball, Your Majesty. And she has not sent word about her whereabouts, but Prince Rene's security detail said he relieved them of their duties in the early hours of New Year's Day and has not reappeared either. So we suspect the two incidences are most likely linked,' Arne finished.

Isabelle's heart sped up. 'What are you trying to say?' she managed, her already agitated stomach starting to churn. Why was Arne behaving as if this were all perfectly normal?

'Ms Taylor and Prince Rene were photographed leaving the ball together, Your Majesty. He dismissed his security detail it is believed to escort Ms Taylor back to Androvia alone.' Arne cleared his throat, a dull red staining his cheeks, confusing Isabelle even more. 'But when they didn't return to Androvia it was assumed they...' He trailed off.

'For goodness' sake, Arne, please just say whatever it is.'

He coughed. 'They decided to have an assignation together.'

Disbelief came first, swiftly followed by a new wave of anxiety.

'As you know, Prince Rene has a tendency to...' Arne

continued in that strained tone '…disregard his schedule when he is in the mood for…female companionship.'

'That's not possible,' Isabelle cut into Arne's painful explanation. 'Mel would never go off with Rene.' Because she hated him.

For the first time, fear gripped her throat.

'Are you telling me no one has seen either one of them since they left the ball three days ago?' she demanded.

'Well, not specifically,' Arne announced. 'But I have been assured by Prince Rene's private secretary it is not at all unusual for the Prince to be unavailable on occasion.'

Isabelle simply stared. She'd known Rene was troubled, and that he struggled with his role, but she hadn't realised he went AWOL on a regular basis.

'I don't care if it's not unusual for him,' she said, knowing that while Rene might be extremely unreliable, Mel certainly was not. 'It's utterly unprecedented for Mel to disappear without a word. We need to contact the police,' she said, her fear rising. Mel simply would not do something so irresponsible as to go off like this, especially with a man she could barely say two words to without starting an argument. 'And start a search for them both.'

Arne's eyebrows rose. 'But, Your Majesty, that will create unnecessary press speculation. And be an embarrassment for the Saltzaland monarchy.'

'I don't care if it's an embarrassment,' she shouted, forced to raise her voice. Why wasn't Arne listening to her?

'Hey, Belle, what's all the yelling about?'

Isabelle turned to see Travis leaning against the door frame of her office. Relief flooded through her at the sight of him—so tall and indomitable—and the wild rush of pleasure followed… He had called her Belle. Her heart bounced into her throat. Stupid to think she had missed that silly nickname so much, too. But before she could find the words to explain to him why she was so anxious, Arne bowed deeply and began speaking in that patronising tone again.

'Your Highness,' Arne said, addressing Travis. 'The Queen is concerned about the whereabouts of her personal assistant, Ms Taylor, but I have assured her there is nothing to worry about.'

'Arne, I think I should be the judge of that…' she began, becoming increasingly annoyed with her courtier. He had always had issues with female authority, but she had never had her direct requests countermanded before.

As Travis pushed away from the door and walked towards them both, the flood of yearning only increased the emotional turmoil inside her.

What was happening to her? Why was she so happy to see him? *Was* she overreacting? As Arne suggested? She didn't think so—her concern about Mel was totally justified. But somehow the sight of Travis was playing havoc with her composure, as well as her convictions. Especially when he reached her and she got a lungful of that familiar scent. The yearning surged, but right alongside it was the foolish feeling of hope that had been crucifying her for days now.

'I want you to contact the police, Arne,' she said to her chief courtier again. 'There is no need to contact the media as yet. But we may need to arrange a press conference if the two of them cannot be found,' she said, determined to ignore her overwhelming reaction to Travis's nearness to focus on the problem at hand.

'But, Your Majesty—' the courtier began again.

'Arne, do what she tells you,' Travis interjected, the commanding tone brooking no argument.

To Isabelle's relief Arne bowed again, finally having got the message. 'Yes, Your Highness,' he said to Travis, before leaving the room.

But as the office door closed behind the courtier, and she found herself alone with the man who was not supposed to be her real husband, the relief twisted inside her, becoming hard and jagged. Why did she feel so weak and needy all of a sudden? She shouldn't rely on Travis's support. Any more than she should be grateful Arne had listened to him and not her—when she was his queen, and Travis wasn't even a real consort.

'Okay, so what's the problem? And why do you feel you need to involve the police?' he asked. But she could see the shuttered look in his eyes that had made her feel so alone in the past few days.

'Mel has gone missing,' she said, retreating behind her desk, her feelings far too close to the surface. 'She and Rene haven't been seen since they left the New Year's Eve Ball, which I forced her to go to in my stead,' she added, the guilt washing over her.

Travis propped his hip against the desk and crossed his legs at the ankle, the casual stance displaying a confidence she had never felt around him.

Why was this so easy for him? When it was so hard for her?

'So why isn't Arne concerned?' he asked.

She sat down, and stared out of the window onto the gorge, determined not to feel intimidated by his relaxed demeanour. Or to second-guess her reaction again.

The snow had been falling since New Year's Day, blan-

keting the country and making travel increasingly difficult.
What if Rene and Mel had somehow got lost in the white-
out? It was a five-hour drive through the high country to
the White Palace from Gaultiere Castle in Saltzaland. And
they would have been driving at night. But when Travis
continued to wait for her answer, she was forced to admit
the other explanation.

'Because Arne—and apparently everyone else on my
staff and Rene's—thinks that Mel has suddenly lost her
senses and gone off on an…' she lifted her hands to do air
quotes '…an "assignation" with a man she has never liked.'

Travis let out a gruff chuckle that stabbed at the heart of
all Isabelle's insecurities. It angered her that Arne hadn't
taken her seriously, but it hurt to see him do it too.

'The Playboy Prince strikes again, huh?' he murmured.

She stood to slap her hands on the desk. 'Don't you dare
laugh, or make light of this,' she said, allowing her temper
to seal up the empty space, at least a little bit, which was
always there now when she was near him.

'Cool it, Your Majesty.' He lifted his hands and levered
himself off the desk, the mocking gesture belied by the hard
glitter in his eyes. 'I'm just offering an opinion.'

'I don't want your opinion,' she said, determined to finally stand up for herself. 'And don't call me Your Majesty when you have no respect for my office whatsoever.'

The hard glitter darkened, the flash of emotion behind
the mask of casual charm somehow vindicating. Until he
spoke.

'That would be the office you use as a shield, so you
don't have to feel any real emotions, is it?' He ground the
words out, his anger as shocking as the chasm opening up
in the pit of her stomach at the contempt in his eyes. 'You're

damn right I don't have any respect for it. But hey, your friend's booty call is not my problem. I only came to tell you I'm heading back to Colorado for a couple of weeks.'

He turned to leave.

'But you can't leave.' She dashed around the desk to grasp his arm. 'I need you here.'

The chasm expanded when he glanced down at his arm, where her fingers gripped the cool fabric of his suit jacket.

She wished she could grab the words back when his gaze met hers. And what she saw there threw her back to her childhood, when she had begged her father to stay, to care for her, and he had looked at her the same way—with pity and impatience—as if she were an inconvenience to be managed, a burden to be handled.

'Aren't you forgetting something, Belle?' he murmured. 'This isn't a real marriage.'

She released her grip on his arm, even as the yearning in her heart sank into the chasm too. Along with the last of her strength and resilience.

As he walked away, without a backward glance, fear and sadness shattered her heart and made her feel like that broken child all over again. Wanting—and hoping for—something she could never have.

'Take me to the airport in Androlov,' Travis demanded, slinging his bag into the back of the cab.

'Your Highness?' The driver seemed stunned as he climbed in.

'The name's Travis Lord,' he snarled. It had taken over two hours to get packed and arrange a flight out of Andro-via—because his company jet had returned to the States—and he needed to leave now, before he lost any more of his cool. 'There's a hundred-buck tip in it if you can get me there in under an hour.'

He'd lost his temper with Belle, something he'd promised himself he wouldn't do. Ever since she'd turned to him in Colorado and told him—in that carefully polite tone—that she really didn't think they should share a bed any longer. And made him feel like nothing.

He got that he'd overreacted. Theirs could never be more than a sexual relationship—they'd agreed to that, hadn't they? But he'd thought they'd eventually become friends during their time together in Colorado. Every time she'd turned to him with need in her eyes, every time she'd trusted him to hold her safely while he'd taught her some moves on the snowboard, every time he'd watched her go over and he'd held her afterwards… It had started to feel like—more.

He still wanted her, sure, but he could get over that. What he couldn't handle though was the feeling of being used.

So, when she'd told him he didn't respect her, he'd let her have it. With both barrels. But he refused to feel guilty about it.

The cab pulled through the gates of the palace, but had to stop on the verge to let through a couple of trucks with a US news channel's logo on.

He glanced over his shoulder as the cab headed out of the royal compound. Then leaned forward to tap on the glass.

The driver slid open the divider. 'Yes, Your… Mr Lord,' the man said, correcting himself.

'What's with the news trucks?'

'They have been arriving for the last hour. Her Majesty is giving a press conference in ten minutes,' the man replied, sending Travis a puzzled look. Probably because he was supposed to know what was going on in his wife's life. That would be the wife he'd just walked out on in a storm of hurt feelings.

*'I need you here.'*

The plea echoed in his skull—as it had been doing for the past couple hours while he'd been slinging stuff into his bag and rearranging his schedule commitments to make his getaway to Colorado—but this time he couldn't seem to convince himself she'd been playing him.

He'd seen the panic in her eyes, felt the tremble of her fingers holding onto his suit—and he'd decided it was all an act. Just like all the other moments when he'd sensed the volatile emotion under the polite indifference.

He couldn't pose as her loving husband any longer. Not until he could stop wanting her, all the damn time. Not until he could get over his obsession with her—which had grown to impossible proportions since their marriage. Not just the constant need to touch her, and caress her, and make love to her... But worse than that, the desire to listen to her voice—so precise, so determined, so honest and forthright—talking about everything from palace business to the crummy way her old man had treated her as a kid—and see the emotions swirling in her eyes. The emotions he had kidded himself she had hidden from everyone but him.

But uncertainty rolled around in his chest, along with the great big boulder that had been lodged there ever since their heart-to-heart on Christmas Day.

He glanced at his watch. Then grabbed his phone out of his pocket, to switch on the local news app. Within seconds, the newsfeed was interrupted for a 'special report' from the White Palace.

The conference had been set up in one of the palace's

many staterooms, the same room he had walked through close to three months ago now.

Isabelle appeared in front of the desk, and the camera flashes went off instantly.

He enlarged the picture, to gauge her expression. She looked demure, controlled, reserved as always. But behind the façade of composure, he could see the cracks. The smudges under her eyes, which he had spotted during their argument but chosen to ignore. The slight tremble in her fingers as she read from a prepared statement.

The words didn't really compute. Something about the disappearance of her assistant, Mel, and the Playboy Prince—the police's concern that not a trace of them had been found.

Guilt made his throat ache, her distress clear to him now. Why the hell had he let his temper stop him from seeing what was so damn obvious?

Maybe because he hadn't had the guts to confront his own feelings, about her.

After the local police chief added his information about the investigation, the palace's press secretary opened the floor to questions. There were a couple about Prince Rene—seemed this wasn't the first time the guy had disappeared without warning—but then the reporters from the international press broke ranks.

'Where is your new husband, Your Majesty?' one of them asked. 'Is it correct that he has left you to deal with this situation alone while returning to Colorado?'

Anger burned in Travis's gut. How the hell did they know about that already? He'd only made the decision to go a couple of hours ago.

But before he could figure it out, the camera closed in

on Belle's face—and what he saw had nausea rising up to replace the fury he wanted to feel, with her, with himself, with the whole damn situation.

That same sick sense of guilt that had crippled him as a kid of nineteen—when he hadn't stood by his mom. Because he'd been so damn terrified of admitting he might need her too.

'He had important business to attend to,' she offered.

But colour rose in her cheeks, and she blinked furiously, to compose herself, the reserve slipping to reveal the vulnerable, devastated girl beneath.

He could feel her struggle to remain aloof, to remain a queen, but he could see the shield crumbling before his eyes and something broke open inside his chest.

*It's not a damn act, Travis, you dumbass.*

She looked so scared in that moment. And he understood finally that it was Mel's disappearance that was freaking her out. Hadn't she told him how much the woman's friendship had meant to her as a kid? She had to be terrified.

But he had refused to see her distress, hadn't acknowledged it, not least because of the little flicker of jealousy at the mention of Rene. But it wasn't Rene she cared about, it was Mel… And it wasn't Rene who she needed with her now, it was him.

Dropping the phone, he leant forward and rapped on the glass. 'Take me back to the palace,' he demanded, his heart rising into his throat. 'And if you can get me back there before this damn presser ends, I'll double the tip.'

# CHAPTER SIXTEEN

'ARE YOU HAPPY for Mr Lord to prioritise his business over the needs of Androvia and the monarchy?'

'Why would he leave you in a time of crisis?'

'Is your marriage already in trouble, Your Majesty?'

Isabelle stood dumbly, unable to speak, while the questions—intrusive, cutting, painful—were fired at her from all angles.

Everything had moved swiftly once the police had been informed of the disappearance—and had ascertained after triangulating Rene and Mel's phone signals that both mobiles had been dead for since New Year's Day. A press conference had been called to ask for information, and Isabelle had insisted she participate.

In many ways, she had welcomed the activity, not just because she was becoming increasingly anxious about Mel and Rene's whereabouts, but because she did not want to have to process Travis's absence, or his parting words.

She was processing it now though. The chasm in her stomach filled with the crushing weight of culpability and regret.

She had brought this on herself by believing she could circumvent the terms of her father's will. Was this why her father had insisted she needed a husband? Because he had seen the weakness inside her, even as a little girl? Had he known then that she would never be loved for herself?

The press secretary stepped in, to try and deflect the questions back onto the subject at hand, but the media—particularly the world media, who had no respect for Androvia's monarchy or its traditions—had scented red meat.

And still she stood—tongue-tied, unable to defend herself or her marriage. How could she, when they were correct, her marriage was a hopeless fraud? And why did it hurt so much to know that, when that was always what it was supposed to be?

Then a commotion began at the back of the room, and suddenly striding towards her was Travis. In jeans and a T-shirt, he looked like the man she had known in Colorado. The man she had fallen hopelessly in love with within the space of one week—like the worst kind of romantic fool.

*He came back.*

She couldn't see the camera flashes any more, couldn't even hear the questions—being shouted at him now as well as her. He strode towards the podium, the crowd parting. Jumping onto the raised platform, he slung his arm around her waist. The heavy weight of it seemed to pull her out of the nightmare and into something even more fraught, even more painful.

*He can't have come back for me. He doesn't love me.*

'Okay, quieten the hell down,' he shouted to the reporters, his deep voice cutting through the furore like a knife. The room fell silent.

'Our marriage is great. I'm here to support my wife.' His arm tightened on her, tugging her against his side in a show of strength, of love, which only made the pain worse. Because she wanted so much to believe it. But she knew it wasn't true. 'Now maybe stop focussing on dumb gossip and concentrate instead on helping the Queen to find two people who matter to her.'

He turned to her and pressed a kiss to her cheek—making the room explode again—before whispering in her ear for only her to hear. 'Let's get the hell out of here.'

She followed him off the podium, the press secretary and the police chief fielding the questions as Travis led her up the staircase at the back of the stateroom, to her library.

But once they were inside the room, away from the media hordes, she gathered what was left of her courage and her strength and pulled her hand out of his.

She walked into the middle of the room, the scent of lemon polish suffocating her.

She turned to find him watching her, with the intensity she had once found so exciting. But it only made the chasm inside her feel more real. And more empty.

'Why are you here? Why did you come back?' she asked, her voice surprisingly firm, given that she was breaking apart inside, because she knew he could only have returned to fulfil the terms of their agreement.

'Haven't you figured it out yet, Belle?' he asked, softly.

She shook her head.

He walked towards her. 'I've done something real dumb,' he murmured, his voice low. 'I've fallen in love with my fake wife.'

He placed his rough palm on her cheek. She reared away from him, even as the fierce yearning gripped her all over again.

'Please don't touch me,' she managed, but her voice broke on the words, shaming her even more. 'And please don't lie to me.'

She might be needy, desperate, delusional, but she refused to let him see her break. Or she would have nothing left when he walked away again.

'I'm not lying, not this time,' he said, his voice implacable, the gaze coasting over her full of admiration and something else… Something fierce and…

She yanked herself back for the second time. But it was so much harder this time.

'All I need to know is do you feel the same way?' he asked.

'Please don't ask me that,' she begged, hating the neediness in her voice. 'It isn't fair.'

The tears rolled down her cheeks, the tears she had promised herself she wouldn't shed. She scrubbed them away with impatient fists.

He stepped forward again and grasped her shoulders to tug her against his chest. That sure solid chest, the steady beat of his heart something she had come to trust.

'Damn it, Belle, I'm sorry. I was a coward.' He wrapped his arms around her. Strong and unyielding, but it wasn't enough to control the fear. 'I knew what was happening between us. It was always more than just sex. But I didn't want to acknowledge it, because it would mean admitting I needed you. And I haven't admitted needing anyone since I was a kid.'

She lurched out of his arms again. The accusation sharp in her voice to hold the traitorous tears at bay. 'I—I don't believe you… You left me, like they did, when I asked you to stay.'

The words spewed out on a wave of vulnerability, leaving her feeling more exposed. But when he grasped her upper arms, and pulled her back towards him, this time she couldn't resist the urge to be held. To matter.

'I know, baby…' He pressed his cheek to her hair. 'Like I said, I was a coward. But if you can forgive me, we can build something better. I swear.'

The bubble of hope pressed against her ribs, but the fear of rejection only made it more painful, more terrifying. 'You have to tell me why.'

He lifted his head, his expression tortured, yet sincere. 'Why what?' he said, but she suspected he knew what she was asking.

'Why did you find it so hard to admit there was more between us?' she forced herself to ask, demanding more from him despite the terrible uncertainty that still remained between them. 'Why did you walk away when you knew I needed you to stay?' She sighed, finally asking the question she had asked once before, and he had refused to answer. 'What happened to that boy, Travis, to make him so sure he didn't need anyone?'

He swore softly, then let her go. She felt the loss immediately. But the hope expanded in her chest when he crossed to the library's tall, mullioned window. And stared out into her kingdom. The kingdom she wanted so desperately to share with him.

'Does it have anything to do with your father?' she asked.

He swung round. 'How do you know that?'

'Because I know exactly what it feels like to never be enough,' she said simply.

He stared at her for the longest time, then he turned back to the view of the gorge. But when he began to speak, she could hear the insecurity in his voice, which he had always refused to share, until now.

'When I was twelve, he came to one of my events. For some dumb reason, I thought he was there for me.' He hitched a shoulder, the movement stiff and jerky and so unlike him. 'And I was overjoyed. I knew I could win—I was the favourite.' He dropped his head, his back so rigid she could feel him remembering the pain of that rejection, and her heart hurt, too. 'I figured if I could ace the field, he'd finally want me. I killed myself that day, took a ton of dumb risks. But what I didn't know was that a couple of the other competitors were his real sons, the kids he was really there to support.'

He shook his head. 'I climbed onto the podium to take the gold, so proud of myself and what I'd achieved and sure he had to be too. In that moment, I had all these wild fantasies, that he would come up to me, that he would offer to be my dad, that he would apologise for never being there for me...' He cursed under his breath.

'My mom was there and she spotted him, too. She saw how devastated I was when he looked at me like I was nothing, as he left with his "real" sons,' he added, lifting his hands to do air quotes. 'It gutted me, that he still didn't want me. But it crushed her, too—which was worse somehow, because she had always been there for me and he never had.' He turned back towards her. 'Ever since then, I made sure never to open myself to that kind of rejection again. It was just me and my mom and we were fine. And when she was gone, it was just me. And that was the way I liked it...'

He headed towards her. His gaze roamed over her face, and made her feel truly seen—not just the competent queen,

but the strong woman beneath, and the vulnerable, terrified girl too—as he always had.

'Until you came along and blew that I'm-the-only-per-
son-I-need crap to smithereens.'

She gripped his hands, held on tight. 'I'm sorry,' she
said. 'Sorry he was so unworthy of you. You deserved a
much better father than that.'

'Yeah,' he said. 'We both did… But don't tell me you're
sorry, Belle, just tell me I haven't spilt my guts for no reason.'

She felt the smile crack her face—at the forthright way
he spoke to her—and the smile reached into her chest to
wrap around her heart. They had a long way to go yet. She
had never loved anyone before, never needed them the way
she needed him. And never trusted that they could love her
back with the same fervour.

But the hope felt worth the pain now. And the obstacles
ahead of her, ahead of them, didn't feel so scary any more,
if they could face them together.

'You didn't,' she said. The tear that edged down her
cheek, though, didn't hurt any more. 'I want to make this
work, to build something better, something that could last.
You mean so much to me, too. I need you with me, Travis,' she said, the hope in her heart obliterating what was
left of the fear.

'Thank God,' he murmured, then covered her mouth
in a furious kiss, which showed her not just how much he
wanted her, but how much he needed her, too.

She kissed him back, with the same fury. The same fervour. But as her mind drifted towards pleasure, her heart
continued to thunder against her ribs.

She drew back, forced to confront the whole truth.

'I want to make this a real marriage, more than anything in the world,' she said. 'To make us a real family. But how do you feel about being Androvia's consort for ever?' she asked.

She loved him beyond reason, but her life was not her own in many ways. And he would be taking on a commitment far greater than simply loving her, if he were to join his life to hers, fully.

She held her breath, scared to hear his answer.

But he only grinned, and cupped her cheek in his rough palm, his expression unguarded, and so full of love she thought she might burst from the sheer wonder of it all.

'I love you, Belle,' he said. 'Your fierceness and your compassion and your determination to see the best in everyone and I especially love that reckless, artless, passionate girl you keep hidden from everyone but me.' He wrapped his arms around her, to hold her close, and pressed his lips to her hair. 'But I also love your loyalty, and your steadfastness,' he murmured. 'And your selfless dedication to this country.' He pulled back, his expression intense, but still full of that charming irreverence she loved.

'I'd like to make it my country, too,' he added. 'But be warned, I'm never going to be great at dealing with the press, or sitting for hours on end listening to boring speeches, or handling all the other protocol and security stuff that goes with your job.' He planted a fierce kiss on her lips, rueful amusement shining in his eyes when he spoke again. 'But if you can handle how crap I am at being a consort, I can sure as hell handle living in a palace and having my wife being the Androvian queen.'

She beamed back at him, so moved by his declaration,

204 QUEEN'S WINTER WEDDING CHARADE

she felt as if her heart were going to explode out of her chest now with sheer joy.

She knew, too, he would be a much better consort than he believed, bringing his own special brand of authenticity and approachability to the role, which she already adored and she knew her subjects would adore, too.

'Understood,' she said solemnly. 'I love you, too, Travis.'

He tugged her back into his arms, his gruff chuckle reverberating in her heart.

But then he slayed her all over again.

'Before we get to grips with any of that, though,' he said, his tone sobering, 'we need to find the rest of your family for you, first.'

'Yes,' she whispered, banding her arms around him and blinking back tears again at the realisation he already understood exactly how important Mel was to her. And how anxious she was about her disappearance. But as he held her, and she listened to the sure steady beats of his heart, she somehow knew they would find a way through this, together.

And whatever it took, he would help her to bring Mel home.

A home that meant so much more to her now, because he was in it, too.

\* \* \* \* \*

*If* Queen's Winter Wedding Charade
*left you wanting more,*
then make sure to check out the next instalment in the
*By Royal Arrangement duet, coming soon!*

*And why not explore these other stories
from Heidi Rice?*

Redeemed by My Forbidden Housekeeper
Undoing His Innocent Enemy
Hidden Heir with His Housekeeper
Revenge in Paradise
After-Party Consequences

*Available now!*